THE LAST DANCE

THE LAST DANCE

SCIONS OF MAGIC™ BOOK EIGHT

TR CAMERON   MICHAEL ANDERLE   MARTHA CARR

DISRUPTIVE IMAGINATION

THE LAST DANCE TEAM

Thanks to the JIT Readers

Dave Hicks
Deb Mader
Kerry Mortimer
Larry Omans
Jeff Eaton

If I've missed anyone, please let me know!

Editor
Skyhunter Editing Team

For those who seek wonder around every corner and in each turning page. And, as always, for Dylan and Laurel.

— TR Cameron

Caliste Leblanc held her sword in a diagonal guard in front of her body, which was positioned in a fighting stance that minimized her opponent's target options. A trickle of nervous sweat emerged behind her ear, traveled down the side of her neck under her red curls, and slid inside the collar of her Def Leppard t-shirt. With a shiver, she glared across the dimly lit space that separated her from her foe.

The Dark Elf had an infuriating smile on her face, one of several that she seemingly had ready at a moment's notice to use in taunting her student. Her unbound white hair fell over her shoulders in strong contrast to her ebony skin. She wore a thin leather jacket that the girl knew from experience was far tougher than it looked and pants of the same material tucked into high boots. The sword she angled in a matching position was slightly shorter than Cali's and single-handed, where hers had enough length to be wielded with a double grasp if desired. At the moment, she desired.

Her muscles trembled. *It's so damned heavy I need two hands. I wish she'd quit tormenting me and start.*

Nylotte slipped forward almost without seeming to move and brought her blade up from below to knock hers aside. She recovered quickly, but the Drow hadn't pressed her advantage. Instead, she said, "You could be dead right now. Perhaps you should devote all your brain to the battle, as whatever portion you've currently committed seems inadequate to the task."

The girl growled inside where her teacher wouldn't hear. *Shut up. You're inadequate.* Fyre, from his position curled on a crate on the far side of the basement, sent amusement over the channel that linked them to tell her she'd "thought loudly" again, whatever that meant. The smile that appeared on the other woman's face gave credibility to her hypothesis that the Dark Ef could read minds.

Cali stepped forward and brought her sword down in a diagonal swipe at her foe and twisted her wrists to sneak the blade under a block. Her target had already slipped out of the way, which left her unbalanced when her weapon failed to connect. She darted ahead and to her left, and the roundhouse kick that would have connected with her skull only managed to disrupt her hairstyle.

She spun and raised one hand off the hilt to cast a ball of force at Nylotte's head. The Drow raised her hand, caught it in her palm, and drained the magic away so its impact was negligible. *And neatly added my power to her reserves. Wench.* The other woman had taught her that skill, but it was nowhere near as automatic for the student as it seemed to be for the teacher. She drove forward again and launched force at her adversary's feet as a distraction while she slashed horizontally at her chest.

Nylotte skipped back but almost immediately stabbed forward. The girl coated her free hand with force and batted the blade away and her mentor disengaged and nodded. "Excellent move, but against some weapons, it might not work. Other magic swords, for instance. It's possible they could be immune to magical shields."

She frowned. "And I assume there's no way to know in advance, right?" The other woman shook her head, and she grinned. "Well, let's test this one. You put a shield up and I'll try to stab you through it."

Her teacher rolled her eyes and attacked again.

They continued with the training for fifteen minutes before breaking to discuss tactics and strategy. The Dark Elf lowered herself into the lotus position to one side of the middle of the circle formed by separate concentric runed rings in the center of the dark basement. She gestured for Cali to sit in front of her. When she tried to set her blade at her side, her teacher sighed as if her student was an idiot. "No, lay it across your legs."

She was sure her confusion showed on her face as she complied, placed the hilt on the right, and balanced the weapon on her thighs. "What's all this, then?" Her attempt at a humorous British accent failed to draw a smile from her companion.

Nylotte shook her head. "It's time for a challenge. You mentioned testing the sword. That is something we must do and there's no occasion like the present."

"I only got it last night. Do we have to do everything

today? I could use a nap." Again, the joke failed. *Okay, fine, be that way.* "What do we need to discover?"

She smiled. "The most important thing of all. Whether the sword will choose to work with you or against you."

"What?"

The Drow nodded. "It's almost certain your sword is sentient. That can be a bonus or it can be a nightmare. If you're unable to convince the blade to be your ally, it will be useless for anything more than hanging on a wall as a symbol of your house's former strength."

Ouch. "Leblanc is stronger than several of the other houses."

Her teacher shrugged. "Perhaps, but it's irrelevant. Eventually, someone will force you into a position where you need to defend against a weapon like that." She gestured at the sword. "And when they do, if you don't have the same bond with yours that they have with theirs, you're unlikely to succeed."

"It doesn't matter. If the house is defeated, so be it. Atreo can come live with me on the surface and New Atlantis can go to hell."

"And what if the sword's cooperation is necessary to free your brother?"

A chill started at her toes and had become a stabbing icicle by the time it reached her brain. The idea that she had yet another thing to do to release Atreo from his magical stasis—other than beating the antidote for the poison out of the Malniets—hadn't even been a tiny possibility in her mind. Nylotte had wrecked the serenity that accompanied the apparent illusion of progress.

"Damn it. Do you really think that's possible?"

Something that hinted toward sympathy appeared in the Drow's eyes, but it flickered away as quickly as it had arrived. "We don't know. Which is why we need to find out. Now, here, and in a controlled way."

Cali sighed. "Okay, tell me what you want me to do."

The instructions had been frustratingly simple. "Connect with the sword. Use your mind, your magic, your spirit, whatever. It should recognize you through the blood-bond you share with the other members of your family who have used it."

"And you know that how exactly?" she'd asked,

The Dark Elf had merely shrugged. "It's simply a guess. But, as someone who uses my entire brain most of the time, my guesses are fairly good." With that, Nylotte had moved outside the circle and brought up each of the shields in turn. When she had asked why a moment before the last barrier snapped into place, her teacher had shaken her head and replied, "Possession is a possibility."

She was now alone with the sword, isolated from the world by magic, and expected to discover how to "connect" with what was, by all appearances, an inanimate object.

Yeah, my life's not weird at all. Not in the least. She sighed and closed her eyes as she placed her right hand on the turquoise gem that adorned the hilt. Her left fingertips slid gently along the blade and explored the runes etched there. Time had not yet permitted the decoding of the marks so she didn't know if they were a message or simply a decoration.

Initially, she channeled her magic into her hands but didn't give it a specific task, merely released it to explore the object. She'd had good luck discovering secrets that way before and thought of it as almost a triggerable intuition. The idea that it might have something to do with her other strange magical sense—the ability to taste intention when she touched people—rose into her mind, only to be quickly banished to a secluded corner. *Concentrate, Cali.*

As her finger traced a rune, she felt a pulse against the magic centered upon the gem. She kept her eyes closed and her senses open, moved her hand to the point of the sword again, and worked systematically down it, feeling the perfectly rounded edges of each rune that ran along the flat of the blade. She took note of those that provoked a reaction and discovered there were nine.

Of course there are nine. Why wouldn't there be? Nine houses, nine districts, nine matriarchs or patriarchs, and nine symbols. Frankly, I'm a little tired of nines.

She packed that thought away as well. They were positioned in such a way that she could touch them all at once. She did so, stretched her fortunately long fingers a little, and pushed magic through them. Nothing happened and with a frown, she tried it again but this time, sent both power and intention into the blade. The result was identical. She sighed, and the motion caused her right pinky to brush against the gem.

Like a sudden portal she hadn't known was there, she was sucked forward and down and the world blurred from the speed at which her consciousness descended into the sword. She landed softly in a patch of dirt that had once probably been covered by grass, to judge from the few dead pieces still visible on the earth next to her face. A quick inventory of her body revealed no damage from the fall or whatever it was, and she climbed first to her knees and then to her feet. She moved to brush her clothes off and frowned when she registered that they were clean.

The barren area seemed somehow familiar, and as she turned in a circle to take it all in, she realized it was strikingly similar to the royal grounds in New Atlantis. With that discovery, the empty landscape all around her began to fill in as if drawn by an artist's pencil, and buildings and a ring road took shape in all directions. When it was complete, she stood in the center of a ruined version of the New Atlantis she knew with a broken palace, damaged or destroyed noble houses, and the faint scent of smoke in the air. The dome above was a spiderweb of cracks that would in no way be sufficient to keep the water out.

"Holy hell," she said. "This isn't New Atlantis. This is the old one."

The startling voice from behind her was deep and masculine. "It was once alive and is now dead. Exactly like you are about to be."

Cali spun and saw two opponents, a man and a woman. Each was at least thirty years older than her, and their faces seemed wise and intelligent. She would have judged them supportive rather than threatening if not for the large swords they held, which were duplicates of the one that suddenly appeared in her hand. With a flash of insight, she recognized them. She'd seen their portraits in the Leblanc mansion. They were the first leaders of the house, dead and buried for centuries. As they strode forward to kill her, her mind had time for only a single thought.

For dead old people, they seem fairly spry.

CHAPTER TWO

Cali lurched to her left to position the woman in front of the man and caught the descending blade on its twin. She circled her weapon outward, deflected the other, and stabbed ahead. The first matriarch Leblanc backpedaled with a grim smile on her face to avoid the blow, and her partner darted in from the right.

She jumped back to dodge his thrust, covered her off-hand in force, and reached out for his blade, intending to trap it and attack him while he struggled to reclaim it from her. At the last instant, she remembered Nylotte's words and yanked her hand away.

He nodded. "Good move, youngster. My sword doesn't care about your magic."

The patriarch strode forward deliberately and swung with measured strokes along all the vectors Ikehara had trained her to defend—almost as if he was testing her abilities the same way her sensei did.

Of course, we don't use edged weapons in the dojo. She willed the bracelet on her left arm to turn into one of her magical Escrima sticks so she could both strike and cast with that hand and was only partially surprised when it didn't respond. *I hate it when other people make the rules.*

Her foe made a particularly clever slash that forced her to dodge left and she threw herself into a roll as the woman slid into view and attempted to remove her head.

She rolled to her feet with a growl. "You two seem like you've done this before."

The matriarch chuckled but the sound was grim rather than amused. "Indeed, against every new patriarch or matriarch who has tried to claim the sword." She advanced cautiously on Cali's left.

The man did the same on her right and clearly tried to get closer without spooking her and causing her to run. He added, "And some who weren't the leader of the house, too, from time to time. Ambitious ones unwilling to wait or who were outside the direct line of succession."

The girl threw a wall of force in the woman's path but she walked right through it. *Dammit. Either my magic doesn't work or they're immune. Whichever it is, I don't like it.* "What happened to them? The ones with more ambition than sense?"

He laughed as he leaned in and swung at her head. She blocked and spun away to evade the woman's follow-up strike. Her foes worked together smoothly, which suggested they had indeed played this game many times. "It didn't go well for them. Let's leave it at that."

She frowned. "So they weren't able to use the sword after, is that it?"

The woman suddenly increased speed and chopped down at her. She raised her blade to intercept, and her foe used it as a fulcrum to drive the pommel of her weapon into Cali's face. She staggered back with a cry of anger as her eyes filled with tears from the blow. Frantic swipes of her sword kept her opponents out of attack range as she recovered. "That was nasty."

The first matriarch laughed. "You can't fight fair, Caliste. That's what your enemies expect. Sometimes, you have to get dirty when you're battling against filth."

Her vision cleared and she brandished her blade warily before her while she kept them both in focus. "How about you answer my other question?"

The man nodded. "They couldn't use the sword, that is correct. But they also lost some of their magic, which was drawn inside to keep Defender empowered."

"Defender?"

He gestured at her hand. "The name of the Leblanc family sword is Defender." He used her moment of distraction to advance in a smooth glide that brought him into range. He slashed abruptly and she met it with a high block. Her foe disengaged and circled his weapon for a straight thrust, and she twisted to the side to avoid it instead of meeting his force with her own. She skipped in and delivered a sidekick to his ribs while she held her blade interposed to prevent him from cutting her. He made a loud huffing noise and she thunked her hilt down on his hand to knock his sword free.

Cali kicked the pommel and the weapon spun away. Unfortunately, it scraped directly toward his partner, who lifted a boot and stamped at the perfect moment to stop it. She stooped, picked the sword up, and twirled one in each hand like it was her preferred style of fighting.

With a sigh, the girl asked, "Do we honestly need to continue this? I'm not ambitious and I am the head of the house. Can't we simply...you know, agree to work together?"

The other woman raised an elegantly sculpted eyebrow. During the pause, Cali took stock of her foe. There were some wrinkles but not that many. *She looks more like fifty than three hundred and fifty or so.* Her straight red hair, a shade darker than Cali's, was bluntly cut at the level of her chin. Her cheekbones were sharp and perfect, which inspired envy. She spun the swords as if the weight didn't bother her at all, while the younger woman's arms were already aching. "Sure we can. After you've proven you're worthy of more than donating your magic to Defender's reservoir."

"It wasn't exactly the answer I was hoping for." She set her feet into a back stance and raised her blade to guard position. Fortunately, she and Ikehara had done some training with two blades against one. She would unquestionably have to up her game before she fought the Malniets, though, since they'd no doubt bring the best of the best.

The other woman shrugged and attacked. Cali twisted away and the man stood at the side, his arms folded and a grin on his face. He resembled his partner, she suddenly realized, enough that they were probably parent and child. Either he was older or had gone prematurely grey, as his short-cropped hair was all the shade of light ash.

Her evasion dealt with the first cut, but the second sword lashed at her back.

She raised her blade and stabbed it along her spine to catch the incoming blow with a resounding clang. When she kicked back, she caught only air and dove forward to avoid whatever the other woman was doing. The swords whistled through the space behind her and she came up running. Sensing her adversary's close pursuit, she feigned a hitch in her leg and leaned to that side, then used the motion to make a fast twist. Her sword arced along a horizontal plane at neck height.

The older matriarch caught it between both her blades and yanked it down and reflex took over. Cali released the weapon and launched a jump kick while her foe's guard was down. Her foot snapped into the woman's chest and thrust her back. The girl stayed close so the swords couldn't intervene and launched punch combos to her enemy's midsection, followed by an uppercut to her jaw. Her opponent landed hard on her back and the weapons fell out of her hands. She raised her arms to cover her face and shouted, "You wouldn't hit an old lady, would you?"

The younger woman stared at her incredulously, and both her adversaries began to laugh. The man approached and she gathered the swords and moved to a safe distance. He ignored her and helped his partner to stand.

They both turned to regard her with smiles before he said, "Well done, Matriarch Caliste. You have earned the right to wield Defender."

She tilted her head to the side, confused. "But I didn't defeat you with my sword."

The other woman shrugged. "That wasn't the point. We don't care about skill but what's in your heart. On behalf of the others, we have recognized you as one who shares our principles."

"You can tell that by how I fought?"

The man gestured toward her. "Everything you need to know about a person is there to be discovered by watching them fight."

Cali's confusion seemed to only increase and it was time to put a stop to it. "So we're done?" They nodded as one. "Okay, then, how do I get home?" The woman waved a hand and the forces that had brought her there began to gather around her. Suddenly, something they said penetrated her brain. "Wait, there are others?"

A whooshing sound was her only reply.

The girl opened her eyes and sighed at the sight of Nylotte's basement. The surrounding shields fell and Fyre was instantly at her side and rested his always shockingly soft scales against her bare arm. The sword lay across her legs but felt different than it had. Like it now belonged to her as opposed to something she simply wielded because it was in her hand. She looked up as the Drow sat opposite her. "You might have warned me."

Her teacher chuckled. "Of what? I had no idea what to expect. You're the first student I've ever had who's also the matriarch of a noble house that possesses an heirloom sword. I have considerable knowledge but I don't know everything."

Cali shook her head. "Uh-uh. You won't get out of this that easily. Surely you're aware of how other people with sentient swords have interacted with them. You could have maybe mentioned the whole fighting for credibility thing."

The Drow's expression turned inquisitive. "For credibility, you say? Usually, it's for dominance."

"Ah-ha," she almost shouted. "You did know and you said nothing."

Nylotte flashed her a wide grin. "I could never steal the joy of self-discovery from one of my students. So, what's the sword's name?"

"Who says it has a name?" She hoped she sounded less petulant than she thought she did.

The Dark Elf rolled her eyes. "Of course it has a name. All of them do. Cara's daggers are Angel and Demon. Diana's sword is Fury. I've never come across a sentient weapon without a name."

"So you've been around others?" Her teacher nodded. "And you still didn't tell me? You suck."

The woman raised an eyebrow. "So I've been told. Will you keep the name secret like some kind of whiny child?"

Maybe I will. Fyre snorted and Cali sighed. "No. I won't keep the name secret. It's Defender."

The reply was sarcastically condescending. "How noble." But the emotional distance between them faded as her mentor smiled again and she sensed the concerned goodwill in her tone. "Now, we need to discover how it can best serve you by trying everything I've ever heard about a magic sword and what it's able to do."

Cali fell back on the stone floor of the basement with a groan. "You mean we need to do that after I've had a nap, and food, and maybe a good night's rest, right?"

The words she'd feared were imminent were tinted with the Drow's typical wry humor. "There's no time like the present. Quit complaining and get up, Matriarch."

Fyre's laughter filled her mind, and she levered herself to a seated position with a groan. "You'll pay for this. Both of you. A horrible, horrible price." The fact that the Draksa's mirth only increased told her the threat, as hers most often did, failed to worry its recipients in any way whatsoever. *I really need to get better at that.*

CHAPTER THREE

Ozahl stepped through the portal onto the docks of New Atlantis and looked around in satisfaction. "It's been too long since I was here for any useful length of time and far too long since we were here together."

Danna Cudon took his hand and squeezed it. "But soon, we'll be able to do what we want, when we want, and where we want. Including New Atlantis."

He glanced at the love of his life and nodded with a smile. She'd dressed down for the occasion and had traded in her normal suit and tie for a simple pair of jeans and a sweatshirt. Her typical slicked-back hairstyle had been replaced by one that allowed the straight locks to fall where they would, and it was dyed strawberry blonde to hide her recognizable ebony hue. To him, she looked amazing, as always. To those around them, she would be merely a face in the crowd, which was the point of her choices.

His transformation had been even easier. He'd cast an illusion to alter his features into an imitation of a businessman tourist he'd once seen. Below that, he'd used makeup and hair dye to alter his true appearance in case anyone penetrated the magic. His clothes matched hers. They had no doubt that the man they intended to visit would identify them quickly—you didn't play games with patriarchs and matriarchs without assuming they would use all the resources they had to hand. But the rest of the city could stay ignorant of their identities.

For now, until we return as the leaders of a new noble house. They hadn't decided yet who would take the titular role and be burdened with political duties. Playful arguments generally devolved into denials of any desire to do the job. Despite that, he knew she was as ready for it and as eager to do it as he was. He shrugged mentally. *We might have to flip a coin in the end.*

Ultimately, which of them led wouldn't matter. Claiming one of the nine noble houses was the only thing that did. *Well, and surviving to enjoy it.* That's why they now visited the underwater city. Their primary route to becoming New Atlantean nobility required Caliste Leblanc to defeat House Malniet and leave a power vacuum in her wake, as she had no family ready to step in and take the vacant place.

The mage shook his head to banish the thoughts and returned his companion's hand squeeze. "Right you are, my love. Now, it's time to make a patriarch unhappy."

Danna released her grasp and produced a coin for one of the runners who were always available on the docks, young folk from the surrounding settlements who would never be able to afford to live in the domed city, no matter how many menial tasks they performed. He had been like them once, as had she. They'd both known they were destined for more and when they'd found each other, they had decided that together, they could rise very high indeed. He followed, and they climbed the stairs side by side.

"So, should we stop for food?" she asked. "Some light shopping?"

Ozahl chuckled. "You paid that girl to tell the patriarch we'd be coming immediately."

"Yeah, but it's not like he'll see us immediately. And if he does have to wait, anger can be a useful lever."

He shook his head. "We need to keep our eyes on the prize here and you know it." Her grin told him she did. "You're only screwing with me."

Her laugh held no worry. One of the things he most loved about his partner was her capacity to truly live in the present. Others might be concerned about the events they were about to set into motion, ones that bore the very real danger of having a price placed on both of their heads. *Because Styrris Malniet never does his dirty work.* But not Danna. She had the ability to flow from moment to moment without any baggage at all when she chose to, and he envied that skill. She nodded. "Of course. You can't be serious all the time, love. It's not good for you."

"Maybe now is an appropriate juncture for seriousness? Given the gravity of the situation?"

She shook her head. "This is when it's least useful. I think you need a drink before we do this. I know I do. Let's get a move on since we wouldn't want to keep dear Styrris waiting for too long."

They'd stopped for a single glass of liquid courage at a bar that was along their path to the Malniet mansion. Thereafter, they took the first ring road on their route to reach the appropriate spoke heading toward the center. Taking the circle that ran around the palace would have been more efficient but would also have made them very visible to many more noble eyes, something that wasn't to their benefit at the current moment.

Danna clearly thought along the same lines because she broke several minutes of silence by observing, "Soon, they'll all know who we are and will condescend to us at their own risk."

He nodded. "Soon. But not yet, unfortunately."

Discussing plans wasn't necessary as they were both very clear on their objective and the possible ways to reach it. When they talked, it was therefore of insignificant things—this piece of architecture, that piece of greenery, and the kind of parties they might host when they were part of the city's upper crust. The comfortable conversation kept them occupied until the moment when they arrived at the front gate of the tall metal fence that bounded the Malniet property. It was closed and two guards stood inside.

Danna nodded briskly at each of them. "We have an appointment with the patriarch."

The one on the left made a show of scrutinizing them lazily. "That seems unlikely," he drawled.

"Nonetheless, we do," Ozahl replied.

The other guard responded with a frown. "Come back when you're appropriately dressed for an audience."

Danna laughed. "An audience, is it? It sounds like

someone thinks they're a monarch, rather than merely one of nine nobles."

The property's defenders bristled at that and perhaps even considered emerging from the safety of their metal enclosure, but the situation was saved by the appearance of a servant in formal attire. "You are welcome at the Malniet estate, Ozahl and Danna," he intoned. "Your runner described you both quite well." To the guards, he snapped, "Open the gate."

They leapt to obey, all traces of condescension replaced by fear. *Apparently, the majordomo or whoever this is wields a fair amount of power. That's good to know.* The man introduced himself. "I am Charles. Please come this way." He turned to lead them into the house. As they walked, Ozahl noted the unusual thinness of their escort, a look he'd formerly only associated with addicts and the poor. This person was unlikely to be the latter, but if he was the former, it presented…possibilities. He filed the information away at the back of his mind as they entered the mansion.

The entryway was opulent, with staircases that led up on both sides to a second level and a hallway that stretched down the center of the space. The servant led them down it and they passed numerous closed doors before they emerged into a sizeable living room. It was equivalent to half his apartment and held three couches, a love seat, several tables, bookshelves, and a large cabinet filled with alcohol and beautiful glasses for serving it.

On one of the couches, clad in a business suit that would likely make Danna jealous of its fine quality, was the man himself with a book open on his crossed legs. Styrris

Malniet was the perfect example of what a wealthy zombie might look like—tall, thin, and with protruding cheekbones under short dark hair. On the rare occasions when he'd seen the patriarch before, the man had worn a longer style. One could read anxiety into the new choice but that would be assuming a little too much. Styrris was an individual who knew well how to manipulate others, and such slight touches would be a part of his repertoire. *Exactly as they are of mine.*

He looked up at their arrival but did not deign to rise. His voice was low and rough. "Your messenger said you had information for me that would be, and I quote, 'vital for the survival of my house.' If I find you are wasting my time, I will see you both destroyed for your impertinence."

Ozahl bared his teeth in a false smile and forced his natural aggressive response down in favor of a measured reply. "Of course, Patriarch, we would never seek to waste your time. The information we bring is indeed vital, both to the survival of your house and your person."

His host raised an eyebrow. "One could interpret that as a threat."

Danna shook her head. "That is certainly not how it's intended, Patriarch. We have no desire to threaten you, only to share what we know as well as an opportunity."

Styrris sighed, closed his book, and placed it on the couch beside him. "I'll give you five minutes."

They'd decided Ozahl should be the primary speaker and predicted that the patriarch would respond better to a man, given that his current nemesis was a woman. "Then we'll be brief," The mage said. "You have a problem and her name is Caliste Leblanc. Doubtless, you think you have her under control, but many others thought the same, only to discover their error too late to save themselves. We would hate to see you make the same mistake."

The patriarch snorted softly. "The girl is nothing. A nuisance."

He smiled. "As the others before you believed. And yet, she has won every battle she has fought, most recently against a superior force you sent to kill her. Outside the rules of ritual combat, I might add."

"The girl has already invalidated those rules by making an alternate proposal."

"So I've heard." He nodded. "I've also heard you haven't accepted. Either way, it doesn't change the fact that she is resourceful beyond all expectations. However, we know a time when she will be vulnerable, which would give us an opportunity to remove this problem for you."

"The Atlanteans on the surface have a final combat to resolve with the girl," Danna explained. "We, too, would love to see her dealt with outside the rules to avoid any risk of her victory. But since that would also serve your needs, it's only appropriate that you should share in the cost of such a thing."

"And so we've come to make you the offer," Ozahl added. "Our part is finishing the girl. Your part is giving us the resources we need to do it and a particular reward thereafter."

The Malniet patriarch rolled his eyes, but his body language suggested he was interested. The mage's constant use of illusion had taught him to recognize such signals. Unfortunately, the other man didn't display enough of them to suggest he was sold on the idea. "So, for the sake of conversation, what reward are you seeking?"

This was it. This was the moment. His mouth was suddenly dry and he had to force the words out. "House Cormier."

The older man laughed. "What?"

Danna folded her arms and fixed her gaze on Styrris. "You heard him. When you wed Matriarch Cormier, you will gain control of that House. In order to save your own, you grant it to us, free and clear of any obligation."

His laughter was filled with mockery and condescension and made Ozahl's hands clench into fists. "Street trash elevated to the nobility? There's enough of that in House Leblanc already, thank you very much. We don't need more." He shook his head. "And there, for a moment, I thought you wouldn't be a waste of time." He picked his book up and raised his voice. "Charles, have the guards see them out."

They were beyond the front gate in less than a minute, the metal clank of it being secured behind them the ultimate word on their proposal. Danna looked at him and shrugged. "It's not anything we didn't expect."

He nodded. "We tried. Now, we'll have to do it the fun way. I guess it's time to start eliminating his potential champions to ensure that when he does face Caliste, he has less support."

She smiled. "So…if she loses to us or to him, we take Leblanc. If he loses, we take Malniet."

"Yep."

"Well, as the brains of the outfit, I've done my job. Now you do yours and eliminate his support system."

Ozahl laughed. "And why is that my task? You're very handy with weapons and magic yourself, you know."

Danna grinned. "Because I need to find out how to defeat her. Think about it. If we're smart, maybe we capture her house first and then finish Styrris off as a bonus. Usha might like to be a matriarch. Why settle for only one when we can have both?"

CHAPTER FOUR

Zeb ran a bar mop over the wooden surface in front of him to deal with a spill and carefully avoided scowling at the gesticulating wizard who had knocked his glass over. The stresses of the recent events in New Orleans had rippled through the non-human communities and were in evidence among his customers. First, the new drug in town, then the weakness that spread through its users, capped by the battle between the Atlanteans and the Zatoras. Plus, of course, the attack on a member of the magical council. They'd tried to keep that secret but naturally, word got out in no time.

The dwarf shook his head and muttered curses under his breath. *People need to learn to get along, is what it is. As soon as there's a crisis, everyone splits apart instead of coming together.*

He was distracted from further musings by the arrival of Tanyith and Kendra, who took their customary positions with their backs to the door. He considered it a compliment to the tavern that they were willing to do so.

Throughout his time as owner, he had intended the Drunken Dragons to be neutral ground and it had served that purpose quite well, even through the current upheaval. He hoped it would continue doing so long into the future.

Some might argue that hosting council meetings in the basement like the one scheduled for later that evening was a violation of the very concept of neutrality. He would contend it was a way for him to stay on top of what was going on so he knew enough to help maintain the proper balance—or at least keep it from tipping toward the side he considered wrong.

So maybe not strictly neutral. Well-meaning, anyway.

With a welcoming nod, he pointed at the cask that held his special brew. They responded with nods of their own, so he pulled three glasses of the powerful cider and joined them in the corner. They tasted it and complimented him, as was appropriate. "So, what's the situation with you two?" Zeb asked. "Still happily homemaking?"

Kendra laughed. "I haven't kicked him out yet if that's what you mean."

Tanyith shook his head. "Nor I, her."

She swiveled toward him with a mock glare. "It's my apartment."

"No, it's now our apartment. You invited me, or have you forgotten that already?"

She snorted. "After you basically begged me to."

He laughed. "That's not how I remember it."

The proprietor chose to interrupt before they got too distracted. "So, everything is working out, that's good. What about the other thing, Tay? From downstairs?"

Tanyith ran a hand along his slicked-back dirty blonde

hair, which was pulled into a ponytail. He'd managed, finally, to find a suitable length for his mustache and goatee and looked quite reputable in his t-shirt and sports coat. He was the light to Kendra's dark, as her clothes, hair, and makeup all tended toward that side of the spectrum. You'd know she was a cop even if she didn't tell you. It simply radiated from her.

"Well," he said, "as I reported to them—by messenger of course—there's been a slight delay in part one of the plan. It turns out that burning a building down without getting caught is rather more difficult than it initially appears."

The dwarf chuckled. "Imagine that. Especially when you don't want to do it in the first place, I bet."

He pointed a finger. "Exactly." Representatives of the Malniet family thought they had the man on their hook and had demanded he incinerate the Shark Nightclub, the home base of the local Atlantean gang. "Part two, giving them intelligence on the council is going quite well thanks to you."

"I'm happy to help." He'd supplied a steady flow of genuine information about issues of no consequence and false information about the things that mattered. The delaying tactic wouldn't last forever, but things were coming to a head anyway, so that wasn't a huge concern. "And the third item?"

The man shrugged. "We haven't been in any combat yet where I could deliberately allow myself to be disabled and abandon Cali. I doubt they'll want me to do it during the fight with the Atlanteans—or that will be my excuse, at least, when I don't. Then, when I double-cross them in the battle against the Malniets, it should hopefully come as a tiny surprise."

Kendra scoffed. "You can't honestly imagine they believe you'll do it."

Tanyith laughed. "They think I love you too much not to."

"Fools."

"Right?" He shook his head at her. "With your resources, plus the magical council keeping an eye on you and Sienna, the risk is minimal. They've been in their little world for too long and forgot that other people can call in allies, too. At least those who aren't such incredible bastards that they have to resort to extortion to get help." He shrugged in Zeb's direction. "There isn't much to do now but wait for the night after next when we fight the Atlanteans for all the marbles."

The detective growled annoyance. "You should let me show up instead and arrest all of them."

He sighed. "On what charges? You're the one who lives inside the rules, remember? Well, mostly inside."

Zeb stretched across the counter to tap the scowling woman's hand. "There's no need to worry. As long as he doesn't go down in the first wave, I'll keep an eye on him."

She looked at the battle-ax hanging above the bar. "I'll hold you and Valerie to that promise." She twisted and punched Tanyith in the shoulder. "So don't you lose right off the bat, nitwit."

The dwarf shook his head and laughed as the two returned to their verbal sparring. *They really do make a cute couple.*

The preparations for the council meeting were the same as usual, and he was ready in good time for Malonne's arrival, whose wardrobe for the day was a precise suit that seemed almost martial. The pale-skinned and light-haired Light Elf greeted him frostily, apparently still annoyed that the group hadn't shared his opinions about how much and in what way to help the humans. *That's why we vote, so bad ideas are hopefully left behind.*

When the others had gathered, he settled into the seat between Delia, the witch, and Brukirot, the Kilomea. Scoppic, Cali, and Invel had arrived together. She'd gone upstairs to hang out with Tanyith and Kendra, and the gnome and Drow had taken their places at the table.

Vizidus's normally unkempt grey hair was bound in a ponytail, and he seemed to have de-aged with the increasing chaos in the city. He smiled at those gathered around the table. "Thank you all for being here, especially those coming from New Atlantis." He nodded at the two in question. "And, as always, thanks to Zeb for hosting us." Invel lifted his glass and gave the dwarf a grin that he returned in kind. The wizard continued. "Tonight, we have only a couple of items to discuss. First, reports on what's taking place in your communities. Second, plans for the future."

Malonne snorted and spoke out of turn. "So, nothing big, then."

The leader of the council chuckled and tilted his head toward the elf who had interrupted him. "That's certainly a matter of personal opinion. I would say this is perhaps the most pivotal moment we've had in decades here in New Orleans." He turned to Brukirot. "How fare the Kilomea?"

The giant folded his arms and shrugged. The movement made the tight brown leather top he wore stretch audibly. "The same as always. Give me a name, and I will cut the head off any future trouble." He'd made that argument for weeks and as yet, the council hadn't let him off the leash. Zeb had a feeling that might change tonight.

The wizard addressed him next. "And the dwarves and the humans you know?" The dwarven community was comparatively small and generally uninterested in group activity. They trusted him to work in their interests as none of them wanted to be involved with anything other than their own pursuits. He was also able to share the humans' perspective due to his proximity to many of them in his role as tavern owner.

"The dwarves are as they always are," he replied. "They would join us in any activity at need, as long as it was truly a need. Among the humans, the prime item of concern would probably be the upcoming battle between Caliste and the Atlanteans if they were aware of it."

Vizidus nodded. "And that concerns us as well, no question. Delia?"

The dark-haired witch wore a white concert t-shirt with the collar cut off, and when she shrugged, it revealed the strap of a black tank top beneath. "My people are good and at least two of them have eyes on the man's girlfriends at all hours. I pay them a reasonable wage and I'll expect to be reimbursed."

Zeb held his hand out to her and a diamond rested in

the palm. "Tanyith says thanks and you can give him whatever change is appropriate when the threat is over."

She took the gem with a satisfied grin. "Perfect. There might not be much change."

He laughed. "What will be, will be. Skilled protectors don't work cheap."

"Malonne?" The wizard said,

The Light Elf shrugged. "My people are fine but wish for this all to be resolved so we can discuss the future relationship of magicals and humans in New Orleans. I continue to believe we cannot rely upon them to manage their own affairs, given how horribly they have accomplished that thus far."

"So, no change from you, then," Invel replied and shook his head. "The Drow in the city are fine. We're well-defended."

"As are the gnomes," Scoppic said in response to a nod from Vizidus. "I, of course, am spending my time in New Atlantis and I must say, the research opportunities are amazing. The history is so different from ours." He grinned happily and more smiles appeared around the table. Everyone liked and respected the gnomish librarian.

"And the library?" Zeb asked.

The gnome smiled. "Getting along quite well in my absence, I'm told."

The wizard clapped his hands. "Excellent. That takes care of the present. But we must consider what comes next." He raised a hand as the Light Elf straightened in his chair. "I refer to the immediate future—days, not weeks. We are all aware that a battle is coming, one that pits Caliste against the Atlanteans in the city. I think we can all agree that it would be better for magicals and humans both if she were victorious." Nods greeted the statement. "So, shall we intervene? Brukirot has a plan and the target seems obvious."

"The Atlantean leader," Delia replied.

Vizidus nodded. "Usha, yes. Not only the head of the local gang but the Champion of New Atlantis, which makes her a formidable opponent. Plus, we have to assume her organization will marshal all its strongest forces against Caliste. While we hope she can succeed without our intervention, it is only logical that we should consider whether more action is necessary."

The Kilomea shrugged. "You've given me the name. Now give me the word. She'll be dead by tomorrow night."

The dwarf frowned. He was confident they would win the battle and that stepping outside the rules wasn't required. But a small voice inside he couldn't silence suggested that in this case, the result might justify the means. He shook his head. "I say no. I'll be there to help. There's no way we'll lose to the Atlanteans."

In the end, he was outvoted. Only Invel had agreed with him and even the gnome shared the opinion that this moment demanded an intervention. As the meeting broke up, Vizidus clapped him on the shoulder. "I know this isn't what you wanted but it's necessary."

He shook his head. "So you say. Once upon a time, I would have believed you. Now, I wonder if we lose more than we gain by stepping outside the boundaries."

"We're not the first group in this conflict to do so," the wizard replied mildly.

Zeb nodded. "It doesn't make it right, though."

The man patted him on the shoulder again and headed to the portal area without further comment. The dwarf took Scoppic and Invel upstairs to deliver them to Cali for the trip to New Atlantis. "So, will you be in tomorrow night, girl?" he asked.

She shook her head. "I have things to do down below. I'll be back Saturday but not to work. If everything goes well, though, I'll get a shift in on Sunday."

He nodded and turned to Tanyith. "I guess that means you're up."

With a laugh, he replied, "You've got it, boss."

Cali frowned. "You told me there was another server and didn't think to mention it was him?"

Zeb laughed. "I was afraid you'd feel threatened."

She folded her arms and glared at him. "Sure. I leave town for a while and everyone allies against me."

Kendra nodded. "Well, not all of us." She stared at the detective in surprise, and the woman finished with a grin. "I was already against you before you left."

The ensuing laughter that washed over them all reminded him of how it felt before the danger had become so powerful. He peered at Valerie above the bar with a decisive nod.

And two nights from now, we'll take the first big step to getting things back to the way they belong.

CHAPTER FIVE

U sha had chosen to spend the Friday night before the big battle immersing herself in the atmosphere of her club. She'd booked one of her favorite local bands to play Zydeco and whip the crowd up and had entertained herself by dancing a lot, drinking a little, and being sure to have a word with each and every important person present. The flashing lights and brilliant smiles kept her worries at bay, and the sheer volume of people in the venue made her feel comfortable and safe.

Maybe this should be my new career. It wasn't the first time the thought had crossed her mind and she hoped it wouldn't be the last.

Once she'd completed her rounds among the VIPs, she exchanged pleasantries with most of her other guests and worked her way from table to table into the early morning hours. The band finished at one, and while some people lingered, most headed out and she was able to lock the doors at two. She oversaw the closing down of the cash registers and the storage of the night's receipts in the bulky old-school safe. The metal behemoth lived in a compact space hidden by a false panel in the rear hallway. As always, the act of cranking the large handle to close it always added a sense of final punctuation to her work nights.

She fist-bumped with her bartender, who left her to finish closing up the bar. He'd struggled to find a place for himself in New Orleans after immigrating from New Atlantis. Those folks often found their way to the Shark, both because she actively sought them out and because she had a reputation for helping.

And we'll be able to help so many more once the Empress rules this city. Before, when she'd thought that, it had been filled with hope. Most of that hope was still there but a cynicism she wished she could erase tinted it. Shenni had made eliminating it impossible. She sighed. *It is what it is and doesn't change what has to be done.*

With her nightclub duties behind her, she closed herself into her office and slipped out of the brightly colored dress and high heels she'd worn in her role as hostess and into comfortable boots, jeans, and a sweatshirt. The notion of heading to an after-hours bar or club to maintain the happy glow she had going on crossed her mind, but the need to rest before tomorrow night's battle banished it.

A loud crash, like several tables tipping over at once, sounded from the bar area. She frowned and started toward the noise, then considered that the girl might have decided to step outside the rules and come after her. A push on the concealed button opened the small closet devoted to communing with the Empress, and she retrieved the sword she'd used in every battle on the way to becoming Champion. She drew it with her right hand and tossed the scabbard aside.

Usha approached the main room cautiously and peered carefully around each corner before she moved beyond them. Nonetheless, it took her less than a minute to reach the bar area and only another instant to locate her bartender crumpled on the floor against the stage. The surrounding debris suggested he'd been hurled there with significant force.

Her eyes narrowed when she identified the culprit. The Kilomea was huge—easily seven feet plus—and outfitted for battle in leather clothes that were likely magicked armor of some kind. His boots were heavy and vicious-looking, and knives were sheathed in a frankly ridiculous number of locations on his body. A hilt protruded above his shoulder. Her mind cataloged the threat automatically.

He's probably a lefty from the positioning of the sword. Some of those blades look like they're made for throwing. If those were my boots, there would be razors along the edges, so I'll assume there are.

She growled in annoyance. "Do I know you?" Another of the large creatures stepped into view from outside and locked the front door they must have picked. Sounds from behind her were consistent with a third cutting her retreat off. *As if me retreating was a possibility.* She moved slowly to her right to ensure the latest arrival wouldn't be able to attack her from the rear but didn't take her eyes off the creature ahead of her.

The Kilomea shrugged. "Likely not. But I know you, Usha, leader of the Atlanteans in my city."

A laugh escaped her. "Your city? Says who?"

His reply was completely matter of fact. "I choose to dwell here. Thus, my city. The decision to allow others to break their paths and live as they will doesn't change that."

"So, this is letting me live as I will, is it?"

A condescending grin spread across his wide features. His eyes were dark and menacing under a prominent brow. *Hell, even his face looks muscular.* His skin, too, seemed somehow harder or thicker than it should be. She didn't have much experience with or knowledge of Kilomea, something she now considered might have been a mistake.

"You've crossed boundaries that shouldn't be crossed. Attacking a council member for one," he replied.

She shook her head. "That wasn't me. That was Rion Grisham and I'm the person who took care of him."

"Your explanation doesn't matter. It happened because the two of you chose to oppose each other and to take your fight away from the human cattle and involve the magical community. Involve my people. It was a stupid decision."

"Yeah, well, dearly departed Rion wasn't known for his brains." *And I hope you're burning in hell, Grisham, you bastard.* "Is there any way out of this that doesn't end with us fighting?"

"The council would no doubt want me to offer you such a thing. But no. You die here tonight."

"Three on one?" She looked over his shoulder. "That's cowardly."

The Kilomea shook his head. "They simply bear witness. I don't require their assistance. If I judged you dangerous, I would have hunted and killed you before you even knew I was here."

Usha nodded and twirled her sword. "All right, then.

Let's get to it." One of the advantages she'd had in her quest to become Champion was a keen sense of the battlefield. Her assassin had made a relatively poor choice. Outside, in his element, he would have had an advantage. But there in her club? She knew every single thing about it and had overseen the selection of each bottle and the installation of every light and speaker. All of that would give her an opportunity, eventually. But first, she had to let him think he was doing well.

Stupid brute. No matter how good a hunter you are, you've never sought quarry like me.

She threaded a path between the tables in a deliberate advance and kicked chairs out of the way while her gaze remained fixed on her foe. The Kilomea's lips stretched wide to reveal sharp teeth, and his hands blurred as he drew his weapons. As expected, his first flurry was throwing daggers, four of them pulled and hurled within seconds. She shook her head. *You should have done your research, buddy.* One of her rivals in the Champion ritual had been a master with knives of all kinds, and she'd spent hours upon hours having allies throw things at her to practice her blocking. Now, it was simply ingrained reflex to shift to the side to avoid the one on the left and bring her blade up in a gentle sweep to intercept and deflect the others. Her skill was such that it all appeared in slow motion to her highly trained mind.

Her experience told her his next move would be to reach for the sword with one hand and hope to use it as a distraction to hurl another knife. She'd probably guessed it before the idea registered in his tiny brain. She swatted that one aside as well, circled to her right, and entered the open area created by the flight of her bartender. Her subconscious automatically evaluated his slack form and judged that he was injured but would likely recover.

The Kilomea had his sword out, finally. He wove it in front of him, and the corners of her mouth turned up in a slight smile at the way the colored lights that still illuminated the room played on the blade.

She asked formally, "May I have the pleasure of your name? I always like to know who I'm killing."

He growled. "Brukirot," he said and charged at her. She braced herself and shifted into a back stance with her sword held in a high guard. After three steps, he stopped suddenly and threw a knife he'd palmed or produced from somewhere, or kept hidden in some way. She yanked her head to the side, but the blade sliced along her cheek, nonetheless.

And that's an excellent reminder that maybe your skills aren't quite what they were, Usha. Stop being an idiot.

It still wasn't the proper moment to change tactics, though. She let her magic flow into her muscles to make her faster and stronger and dodged to her left as he arrived. The slash that would have cut her in half passed to her right. He jerked the blade up in time to catch the diagonal slice she tried in response, and the metal rang with a violent chime.

They traded a series of blows, parries, and ripostes as each tested the others' reactions, moving through the empty space and widening it at need when forced against an obstruction. She had to acknowledge that he was good enough to have at least entered the contest she'd won but was confident he wouldn't have lasted through very many rounds.

Usha respected the fact that he stayed calm and centered and matched her attacks with his own, seemingly unconcerned about how long it would take to defeat her. If she hadn't supplemented her endurance and strength with magic, he would likely have easily outlasted her. As it was, he probably still would over a long enough timeline, but she didn't intend to give him one.

She retreated to draw him to where she wanted him to be and reached up with her telekinesis before she yanked as hard as she could. The lighting truss above him plummeted to slam into the position he'd occupied before a lightning-fast forward roll took him out of danger. She admired his decision to come toward her rather than move away from her.

The latter would have been easier but either way, her next action was the same. She extended her left arm behind her and grasped several of the bottles of alcohol stacked on the bar shelf. With perfect precision, she hurled them at her foe and his blade became a barrier of steel as he shattered the incoming projectiles before they could reach him. But slicing him apart with shrapnel wasn't her primary plan, either. The fireball she threw after it ignited the liquor and he turned into a pillar of flame.

Usha still hadn't reached her final move. She stutter-stepped forward and extended her magically powered arm in a perfect thrust, and her sword stabbed through the flailing Kilomea's chest. He fell without a word or any further action, and she cast frost over him to keep him from burning her club down. She swung to face the enemy standing at the door, who she'd kept subconscious track of and who had remained still throughout the fight. "So, are we done here? Or will you break his commitment to a one-on-one?"

He raised his hands and backed out of the door, and she turned as the one who had come in from the rear departed the room the way he'd entered. She shook her head and pulled her phone out.

Danna picked up and sounded surprised when she said, "Did you miss me since we last saw each other a whole hour ago?"

She chuckled. The fading adrenaline had left her a little shaken as always happened when the danger had passed. "I was attacked in the club. Guard yourself and send an ambulance."

Anger replaced surprise as her second in command responded. "On it. I'll be there in ten."

She nodded, put the phone away without replying, and moved to tend to her fallen employee. In passing, she kicked the Kilomea. "And here I thought it was Leblanc coming after me," she said to his corpse. "That, at least, might have been a challenge."

CHAPTER SIX

Cali had spent the night at her apartment with only Fyre for company, a rare occurrence now that she was the matriarch of a noble house in New Atlantis. Awakening in an unfamiliar place had felt strange. She dressed, ready for the day, and knocked on Dasante's door.

Her old friend greeted her with a grin. "What's up, you? I haven't seen you around. Not here and not at the square." A bright white t-shirt set off his dark skin, and his hair had grown noticeably since the days—*was it really only a couple of months ago? It seems like forever*—when they were a fixture among the buskers on Jackson Square. He, doubtless, still spent much of his time entertaining the tourists. She, not so much.

He knelt and ran his hands along Fyre's back. "I haven't seen you either, buddy. I hope you're keeping her out of trouble." The Draksa snorted and rolled over for more attention.

Cali shook her head at his antics and chuckled. "Yeah, we've been busy, no doubt about it. More down below than up here, although you might have heard about the episode in the garden district."

He nodded and rose. "I did and assumed it was you. Word is that some idiots had their heads handed to them."

She laughed at that. "Well, it wasn't quite that easy but sure, that's one way to describe it. If not for Fyre, though, the outcome would have been very different." His ability to share his strength with her had turned the tables on their attackers.

"So, what are you doing here, fancy-person? Slumming with the rest of us to remember how it feels?" His grin stole any offense from his words.

"Yeah, no. Unfortunately, I have a very busy day today. After, things should settle here a little, one way or the other."

He frowned. "Those don't sound like equally desirable choices, based on your tone." It was easy to mistake Dasante's general positivity and phenomenal bantering skills for a lack of intelligence or sophistication, which worked to his benefit with many of the tourists. Those who underestimated his brains due to his gentle nature generally wound up losing the most to him in his sleight-of-hand games.

Cali shrugged. "I guess it's a matter of opinion. If things go my way, the Atlantean gang in town will have to leave me alone and I'll be able to pressure them to stop trying to impose their agenda on everyone else. If they win, at least the fighting is over. I'm not sure it'll be the best time to be a non-magical in the Crescent City, though."

"Well, then I guess you'd better win."

Fyre snorted and she nodded in agreement. "That goes

without saying. I'm off to train with Sensei Ikehara and see if he can give me last-minute pointers. You stay safe, D. Hopefully, once this nonsense and some other nonsense I have going on are resolved, the lizard and I will be able to hang out in the Square with you more often."

He raised a fist to bump the one she offered. "I'll consider that a promise. Go do your thing."

<hr>

She walked to the Dojo and enjoyed the midmorning sunshine. The strangely filtered light in New Atlantis didn't give her the same feeling of warm comfort. Fyre flew above her, hidden by a veil. The emotions he sent were similar to her own. Neither of them felt the need to speak and the mental connection was sufficient to allow them to share this experience.

Maybe it's the knowledge that this could be the last time. Fighting the best of the Atlantean gang has the potential to be way more dangerous than anything I've faced so far. Even the ambush by the Malniets. Cali shook her head to push away the thoughts. She couldn't do anything other than what she was doing, so there was no point in worrying about it. Emalia would continue to work to free her brother if things went wrong, and contingencies were in place for all the other areas of importance in her life as well.

She chuckled inwardly and told Fyre, "You know, if I don't survive the battle, Zeb will be the one who's most hurt. He'll be stuck with Janice—truly a fate worse than death."

The Draksa refrained from pointing out that if she

didn't make it, her friends probably wouldn't either. "Well then, you have another reason to win. You should do that."

As she turned down the alley beside the Dojo, she remembered one of her earliest fights before she'd learned how widespread her particular assortment of opponents was. She shook her head in bemusement at it all as she unlocked the rear door and entered the building.

Ikehara awaited her inside, dressed in his standard uniform of dark pants and a white top secured by a black belt. He had gone from his former crewcut to a fully shaved skull, which made his stern, sharp features seem even more imposing.

She'd worn sweatpants and a t-shirt for the occasion as she didn't intend to stay for the formal class after their individual session. Although she now paid to be his student instead of working to clean the dojo, he had made it clear that she was welcome to continue training one-on-one. Even Nylotte had admitted having multiple teachers could be beneficial, especially since the Drow's fighting style differed markedly from her sensei's.

They exchanged nods and he threw her a bamboo sword. They each twirled their weapons in a warmup, exactly as they always did. The normalcy of it all made her smile.

"I've heard through the grapevine that something big is happening tonight," he said. "Is that you?"

She nodded. "I'm afraid so. The Atlanteans have reached the end of their patience, as have I. We'll resolve our disagreement this evening."

He lifted his sword into a salute position, and she returned the gesture. She matched him again as he stepped into a back stance and shifted the weapon into guard. When he attacked, her mind was filled only with the interplay of their swords, blocking his blows, and waiting for an opening. Her sensei was a master of the art, which made opportunities rare, but when they appeared, she struck fast and caught him on occasion. *There's a definite improvement since our first days of training with these weapons.*

After a sweaty half-hour, during which he switched to double swords while she practiced shifting seamlessly from two-handed to one-handed attacks and defenses, he called a halt and motioned for her to sit beside him on the mat. She pushed her wet hair off her forehead and leaned back to shake the rest of it off the back of her neck. "Mental note. Confine my hair tonight."

Ikehara laughed. "That is a wonderful plan. I humbly suggest my solution." He gestured at his head.

She shook her head. "No way. I like my mane, thanks."

He turned somber quickly, and she realized the moment she'd dreaded had arrived. His voice was low and quiet as he said, "I would fight by your side tonight if you are willing."

Cali closed her eyes. The offer was amazing. Her teacher had volunteered to risk his life on her behalf and fight magicals with nothing more than his strength and skill. She couldn't allow it, of course, but was deeply moved by the sincere offer. Regretful, she forced herself to sit straighter and met his gaze. "Sensei, I can't tell you how honored I am that you would join my fight. But I've failed to find anything that would give you the edge you'd need against beings who use magic."

He nodded. "I understand. I regret that reality."

She laughed but it sounded a little bitter. "Not as much as I do. I would love to have you appear and kick Atlantean tail. But even if we covered you with magic deflectors, they would eventually be overwhelmed."

"And I would then be a liability."

Her expression serious, she shook her head. "If that's all it was, the strength of our team could overcome it. But this is a fight to the death and you have so much life left to live." She gestured toward the front of the room, where the trophies were displayed in a bookcase that also held a single picture of her teacher's family. "And you have students and children who depend upon you."

He sighed. His body language told her that he knew this would be the result but had nonetheless hoped for a different outcome. He rose and gestured with a hand. "Come with me for a moment."

Cali frowned but followed obediently as he led her to the tiny space he used as an office. A box rested on the desk, something she'd not noticed the last time she was in the room. It looked like cherry wood, lacquered and polished with inlays of ebony in the shape of Japanese characters. He swiveled the container to face them and lifted the lid, making the hinges on the rear squeal softly. Inside lay a necklace made of gold links, each about the size of the end part of her pinky. A round pendant with a square hole through the center was attached to them. It was gold around the edges but it had a scarlet face. An image of a dragon in thin gold lines was emblazoned on the red background.

He lifted the jewelry and offered it to her with both hands. "This is a family heirloom, passed down through generations. We've traced it back five hundred years, but the trail breaks there. I personally believe it's older. It's worn only when we are seeking good fortune. I have done so twice—when I asked my wife to marry me and on the day I started this dojo. My wife wore it only when giving birth. I would like you to wear it tonight for your battle." He gestured with the object again and she took it from his hands.

Ikehara chuckled. "It's certainly not magical but it has brought many positive outcomes to my ancestors. If negative results ever occurred, they've been lost to history. Hopefully, it will serve you well."

Surprised and touched, she forced words past the emotions that clogged her throat. "This is an honor. Thank you. More than I can say, thank you."

Her sensei nodded and managed a small grin. "Of course, I'll want it back tomorrow after you've won. Don't disappoint me."

She dashed a tear from the corner of her eye and took a deep breath. "Never, Sensei," she assured him as she lowered the necklace over her head and tucked the pendant into her t-shirt. "I'll do my best to make you proud."

CHAPTER SEVEN

Between the damage from the night before and the need to prepare for the upcoming battle, Usha had closed the Shark Nightclub for the weekend. If she was still alive the next day, she'd have the whole staff come in to clean and prepare the venue for the week ahead. If she didn't survive until then, it wouldn't matter to her anyway.

Tables had been shoved together to support fighting gear at various places in the room, with hers and Danna's set up next to each other on the stage. She looked out over the assembled warriors with a critical eye and came away with the same impression as every other time she'd done it. They should be adequate to deal with the girl and her friends. Once Leblanc joined her parents in the afterlife, the Empress would be satisfied and Usha's responsibilities in New Orleans would be almost complete.

She turned to the woman next to her. Her second in command was dressed in the most informal outfit she had ever seen her wear—tight leather combat pants and high boots with a black tank top. The muscles in her trim arms were clearly defined as she pawed through the pile of equipment she'd tumbled out of a large duffel bag.

"So, we get this done and tomorrow, we clean the club and start the process of securing our city," Usha said. "In a week, we'll be done."

The other woman nodded. Her normally well-styled dark hair was slicked back wet, which suggested that she'd also risen late. *It always makes sense to sleep in before a battle.* She wouldn't have chosen to stay in bed until the early afternoon without the post-fight exhaustion caused by last night's activities, but that was fine. It would make her fresher for the event to come. She chuckled inwardly. *Maybe I should send a thank you note to the council.*

"And after that's finished?" Danna asked. "Stay here and live like the Queen of the Big Easy?"

The Atlantean leader laughed. "No thanks. I assumed you would take over here. I have the Champion's reward awaiting me in New Atlantis." She looked forward to living in the house on the outskirts of the domed city she'd won. The Empress had taken her pledge of loyalty and dispatched her to the surface the next day so it remained vacant as far as she knew. "There will probably be enough work to keep me occupied getting it into proper shape."

Her companion shook her head. "I can't picture it. You don't seem like someone likely to thrive in a quiet life."

She shrugged. "For a while, anyway. I'm sure there's no lack of trouble to get into down there if I find myself bored. That's assuming the Empress doesn't simply send me off with another task." She hoped for that outcome as much as she feared it. Being out of Shenni's favor didn't sit well with her. *Or maybe it's the in-between place I'm in, not celebrated and not disowned.*

The other woman turned to face her squarely. "Are you sure that serving the Empress again is what you want?" The sudden tension in her body made it seem like it was something other than a throwaway comment to pass the time.

Usha nodded. "I swore an oath."

"That carried expectations on both sides. Tell me, has Shenni lived up to her end of that bargain?"

"I hear what you're saying and you're not wrong. That's an open question at the moment. We'll see what happens after tonight, I guess." She rotated and faced the rest of the bar. "What do you think of our chances?" Her chin pointed toward the other four beings who would fight alongside them.

"Not bad, not bad at all. I didn't realize Draksa grew so big."

She chuckled. "Nor did I. Inan has done spectacular work with him, as well." The magical dragon lizard in question was twice as large as any she'd seen before. That gave him an impressive amount of strength because a pile of protective plates sized to fit him rested on the floor next to his sleeping form. Overlapping metallic scales that closely resembled those of his partner made up the handler's armor. Inan spun a trident in his hands, first one way, then the other. *We all have our preferred ways of killing time, I suppose.*

The other two people were a mystery to her. She'd never met them before that afternoon and had no information on them other than a strong recommendation from someone she trusted completely. "What about those two?"

Danna grinned. "My boyfriend suggested them."

Usha snorted. "You trust him that much, do you?"

"I do. With anything and everything, including my life."

"If they're not as good as he says, it might come to that. Do you care to share any useful tidbits?"

Her second in command nodded. "They're twins from one of the settlements around the city. If there wasn't already a functioning Champion of New Atlantis, they would almost certainly be in the running to take that title. The man is Amet and the woman, Zandra."

She rolled her eyes. "A and Z. Creative parents."

Danna offered a fake scowl at the interruption. "Anyway, they are fierce fighters. The best that Ozahl knows of, and he has many contacts. They should be enough to throw the battle our way no matter who she brings."

"So, the mysterious boyfriend has a name. Good. When do I get to meet him?"

"Tomorrow, assuming you live that long."

The Atlantean leader nodded. "Well, that's one more reason to send Caliste Leblanc to her parents' embrace."

***

Zeb had made the uncommon decision to close the Drunken Dragons Tavern for the day, given the gravity of the evening's event. Cali couldn't remember the last time he'd done it or if such a thing had, in fact, ever occurred. That he would do it for her was merely one more piece of emotional weight to help keep her grounded as she awaited the battle to come.

The benches and chairs had been shifted out of the way and weapons and articles of clothing covered the long tables. The setting sun filtered through the windows and glinted off bare steel scattered throughout the room. The sight of her allies brought a warm glow to her spirit. Tanyith and Fyre had been with her from the start, and she knew their abilities and vulnerabilities as well as her own. Zeb prepared in a corner with a quiet air about him that separated him from the rest of them. She guessed he was probably recalling something from the past that allowed him to prepare mentally for the fight to come.

She'd sent away one of the two mercenaries Emalia had hired when Wymarc appeared. Invel had portaled him from the public docks to the tavern, and the patriarch of House Jehenel had looked downright nervous as he ascended the stairs. Fyre had snorted in distaste, the Draksa less willing to forgive the man's political machinations than she was, apparently. Wymarc had stared straight into her eyes and declared, "I was a jerk but I'm able to learn. I'll fight by your side if you'll have me." Since he was unlikely to betray her again, given her enemies' attempt to kill him, she'd accepted with a shrug.

Nylotte's appearance an hour later had been far more shocking. First, the Drow arriving unannounced was always a cause for concern as she never knew quite what her teacher was up to. But her clothes and the weapons she carried were the true surprise. The Dark Elf had flashed that wry grin she always seemed to have ready and asked,

"What? You didn't think I'd let you take on this group without me, did you?"

Cali had stammered some kind of sensible reply—or at least she hoped it had been sensible. In any case, she now had a full team with which to battle the Atlanteans, no mercenaries required. She watched the clock on the wall tick inexorably to the moment of truth and did her best to make small talk. When they were within forty-five minutes of departure, they became serious about their preparations.

She and Tanyith chose to wear the uniforms her parents had left—black tunics above matching pants and boots, with a wide gear belt to cinch the top at their waists. He slipped the magic daggers she'd given him into sheaths at either hip. They would allow him to cast through them but weren't otherwise magical. She had a matching pair on her hips. Defender, her family's heirloom weapon, was sheathed across her back.

The sentient sword could provide her with power during the battle, at least, and might have other secrets still to reveal. There hadn't been a chance to determine all that the blade could potentially do. Her belt pouch contained a glass sphere filled with wicked crystal shards that Invel had gifted to her some time before and a spare healing potion. Paired health and energy draughts rode on each of her thighs. Ikehara's good luck token rested on her chest against her skin. Finally, the charm necklace above her clothes held two fully charged charms, one shield and one light.

During a strategy session earlier in the day, she'd discussed whether they should bring their stun guns. Zeb had nixed that idea in no time and suggested that if they worked against magical defenses, there never would have been a need to create anti-magic bullets.

She'd countered with, "Well, maybe we should carry pistols, then," and the dwarf, Fyre, and Tanyith had all offered separate but equally dire predictions of her ability to use a firearm. Although she had grumbled, they weren't wrong. *One more thing to train on when all this is over, I guess.*

Zeb put black chain armor on with brown leather pieces under it. The ensemble looked well-worn but carefully preserved. The metallic links were small and intricate, and she instantly wondered if he had fashioned it himself. She chided herself for stereotyping because surely not every dwarf was a blacksmith. But then a voice in her head added, *But he did make your sticks, so clearly he knows his way around tools.* He also had magical bracelets, presumably ones he created, but his transformed into axes of wood and metal. *So, he might be a blacksmith, after all,* her internal critic supplied. His huge battle-ax, Valerie, lay on the table near him.

Wymarc wore what looked like leather body armor with reinforced sections at the upper and lower arm, thigh and shin, chest, and back. Separate pieces were dyed in the various colors of House Jehenel, dark purple and pale yellow. Cali thought that if a genuine spark existed between them, which it definitely didn't, he would have made a good boyfriend or whatever. But his presence showed that he was an excellent friend.

Nylotte was all in black, with sword and daggers in the same locations as Cali's. Her apparel also appeared to be leather but far more form-fitting and less bulky than the patriarch's. She had no doubt that the Dark Elf's outfit was magically protected against damage and probably incorporated physical defenses as well.

And Fyre...well, he was his usual self, sleeping on top of one of the long tables instead of behind the bar. She walked closer and poked him once. When he failed to respond, she smacked him. He sighed and opened the eye that faced her. "What?"

She shook her head as the warm fondness that filled her summoned a smile to her lips. "Lazy beast. Get up. It's time."

CHAPTER EIGHT

The venue for the battle was an abandoned industrial shipyard many miles away from the heart of the city. Tanyith had scouted the location when the announcement had arrived and since then, a rotation of off-duty NOPD officers recommended by his girlfriend had kept an eye on it. Cali paid for it out of the gems he'd given her, which she steadfastly resisted asking any questions about. There had been no reports of sizeable groups of Atlanteans setting traps in the days or hours prior to the evening's event.

Of course, that's not to say there aren't single Atlanteans causing trouble in the shadows that they failed to notice. Or under veils. Or a hundred other possibilities. Cali shrugged. Controlling everything was impossible, and she was confident she'd done all she could. That included making sure their portal landed them in a defensible corner. They spread out as they stepped through. A single person she didn't recognize stood in front of them, nodded at their arrival, and lifted a phone to his ear.

While they waited for their enemies to arrive, the

others gazed around at their surroundings and since no one seemed to want to talk, she did the same. They were in a corner of a sizeable dock area filled with warehouses and a large building that contained an enormous, half-constructed fishing boat. Weathered wood planks formed a central zone that connected all the structures. Multiple ramps led into the water, and several one-car-width lanes extended to a larger road that ran behind the buildings.

A portal opened in the middle of the wooden platform to reveal their opposition. She recognized the first two, though, the top people of the Atlantean gang. She'd never seen them outfitted for combat and had to admit they made an imposing sight. The others who followed them through were impressive as well, especially the oversized Draksa and its handler. The other two didn't look like the same kind of soldiers her enemy had used against her before, which was an unwelcome twist. Not that she'd planned for a particular arrangement or anything but having a familiar foe would have made life easier.

Her team moved to select their challengers as the gang members spread apart. Cali and Fyre faded to the right and mirrored the actions of the rival Draksa and its handler. She would have preferred to face the leader, but they'd all agreed in advance that she and Fyre would battle any creatures. Zeb and Nylotte strode to the left and positioned themselves across from the two enemy leaders. That put Wymarc and Tanyith together opposite the two unfamiliar foes.

"This is your party," Cali yelled. "You still have time to call it off."

Usha, on the opposite end of the line from her, grinned

and the scarlet lines she'd painted onto her face stretched and twisted. "Kill them all. There's a bonus for whoever brings me the girl's head."

Zeb summoned and threw his magical axes in a single quick motion and the weapons left his hands the instant they were formed. One hurtled toward Usha, the enemy leader, and the other at Danna Cudon, her second in command. He reached over his shoulder and swung his battle-ax, Valerie, out of her holder. Nylotte conjured a wall of force to intercept the flames that both their enemies hurled at them. When the brilliance of the attack's impact on the barrier had faded, the two were running toward a warehouse on the land side of the dock.

He shook his head and growled his annoyance. "They're smart, anyway. Out in the open, they'd be no match for your magic."

The Drow nodded as she let the wall fall and strode purposefully after their enemies. "True. But inside, they'll have to deal with your fighting skills, which are equally impressive."

"I'm old and slow." He snorted, summoned one ax and returned it to its neutral form, and switched hands on the battle-ax to do the same with the other.

Nylotte chuckled. "I know your history, dwarf. I made a point of looking into it. I'm not sure why you keep it a secret from the others, but don't think you fool me for one instant."

They moved to either side of the double doors that led

into the building. He shrugged. "I have my reasons. I'm aware of your past adventures, too. We seem to have a lot in common."

"Right now, the most important thing we share is the need to subdue those women."

"Not kill them?" He didn't want to be responsible for any deaths, but he was somewhat surprised to hear the very practical Drow echo his opinion.

"I try not to cut off future prospects unless there's no other option. Once we have them captured, the decision is still available. Killing them out of hand removes all other potential paths forward."

"Good. Agreed. So, ladies first." He gestured at the doors.

The Dark Elf laughed and raised her hands to blast the barriers off their hinges and catapult them into the darkness beyond.

* * *

The enemy Draksa leapt into the air, and Frye launched himself after it. Cali was impressed that the beast could fly with all the metal plates attached to it, but the fact that her partner could pick humans up and hurl them at walls at his relatively small size was also rather unexpected. Across from her, the handler spun a trident lazily in front of him. She noted sheaths at his thighs for knives and wouldn't be surprised if he had the lightning web spell handy that a previous opponent had used against her. *Or maybe I'm simply paranoid about lightning webs, given how much they suck.*

His scale armor flexed and rippled as he stalked toward her. She wondered idly if it might be made of actual Draksa scales rather than metal but let the thought fall away. As she advanced to meet him, she drew her sword with her right hand and a dagger from her belt with her left. She raised the knife and channeled lightning through it, having discovered that using a tool gave her even greater control of the unpredictable power. A strand of coherent electricity extended toward him, but he caught it on his spinning weapon, which glowed. *Damn it. He stole my magic to use as fuel.*

He confirmed her assumption when he pointed the trident and launched an uncontrolled burst of lightning in her direction. She drew a large circle in front of her with Defender and grounded the attack harmlessly. Her foe nodded in acknowledgment of the conclusion of their getting-to-know-each-other moment and attacked with a yell.

She evaded the stab of the weapon with a sidestep and positioned her sword to deflect it up and over her as the handler whipped it horizontally at her face and spun to put force behind the effort. As soon as the trident was clear, she skipped in and extended a sidekick, but he had stopped his spin halfway and jumped out of range. The barbed tips of the weapon flicked at her face again and this time, she leaned back to avoid it.

If not for her connection with Fyre, the incoming Draksa attack might have been a concern. He fortunately warned her well in advance as they'd agreed he would do if he had to battle another flying creature. A primary objective of their combat strategy was to trap and eliminate the enemy's airborne element. She evaded another strike from the handler and turned suddenly to engage the oversized lizard that rocketed toward her.

<hr>

Tanyith pelted in pursuit of the two he'd drawn by default. Their foes had made an effort to split up and join the other battles, but he and Wymarc had instinctively moved to cut them off. Rather than fight in the open, the enemy had turned and raced to the large building that contained the partially constructed ship. They were clearly magic-users as their flight was far faster than any non-augmented person could run.

He slowed as the distance increased, wary of the potential for a trick from those they followed. "Did you notice that they move almost identically?" his companion observed. "It's eerie."

Tanyith laughed. "I guess that's a twin thing. But yeah, it's bizarre."

"What's the play?"

They reached the entrance—an unblocked opening in the wall large enough to drive a truck through—and lingered outside and out of view. "They have an advantage if they stay together, most likely. We have to assume they're used to working as a team so we'll have to try to split them up. Naturally, we also have to assume they might have thought of that and planned for it."

Wymarc nodded and clenched his fists. "So we know nothing. Which is essentially par for the course with you people." He grinned. "I'm ready."

Tanyith tilted his head in confusion. "No weapons?" He drew the daggers Cali had given him. They were keen steel he could cast through, which meant he wouldn't need to release them to apply his magic. *It's a big improvement from having to toss my Sai in the air to use power.* The only thing he missed was the defensive capabilities his former knives had possessed but these would be far more effective overall.

The Jehenel patriarch grinned. "I make my own weapons." He held a palm out and an orb of confined lightning appeared inside it. "Or use what comes to hand. I'm flexible."

"Whatever you say, man. Let's do it."

Cali threw herself to the side as the oversized Draksa's claws passed through her former position. He screeched and she imagined he was chiding himself for choosing to try to grasp her rather than attack her with his breath weapon. She pointed Defender at his flapping form and channeled an explosion of lightning through it that extended beyond the blade and wreathed the enemy creature in flickering electricity. She bared her teeth in triumph and anticipated his fall.

Unfortunately, the crackling aura was somehow sucked into the armor plates, which glowed briefly. *Holy hell, it's like that absorbent armor from before.* Fyre unleashed a line of frost past her, which was the only thing that jarred her into motion. She dove away in time to avoid being skewered by the handler's trident, which had come in at an escapable angle only because of the Draksa's intervention. She clenched her jaw in anger and sent to Fyre, *His armor might be able to absorb your breath, too.*

Her partner raced after the heavier Draksa and replied, *So I'll tear him to shreds in the space between the plates. Just because Plan A didn't work doesn't mean they've gained any advantage.*

As she turned to face the armored handler, her eyes narrowed in frustration. "You know, you could walk away," she shouted. "Take your pet with you before you both wind up dead. This isn't your fight, not like it is the others'."

He laughed and his voice was strangely high, which reminded her of the timbre of his partner's screech. "Ah, but it is. I've given my word."

Cali sighed. *Of course it had to be someone with ethics. Of a sort.* "So there's no chance I can dissuade you?" The wash of flame that erupted from his trident toward her was an obvious rejection. *Fine. Be that way.* She grasped Defender in her right hand, conjured a shield around herself with her left, and ran forward into the flames. So far, her adversaries had all proven smarter and stronger than she'd hoped. *Again. Heaven save me from competent enemies.*

CHAPTER NINE

The two Atlantean leaders had separated when they'd entered the warehouse. Dusty crates were all around, many of them broken into by vandals or thieves, which offered a substantial number of places to hide. Usha had stayed low and moved to the left along the bottom floor. Her partner had launched herself into the air with magic and ascended to the loft that covered half the space and served as the home for even more storage stacks.

They had expected and planned for the dwarf as much as they could, based on the information they'd been able to dig up. She knew he had the ability to conjure magical axes that would return to his hands. The impressive battle-ax he carried was probably magic, too. Gossip said he had been quite a fighter in his day but had given it up to become, of all things, a bartender and tavern owner. *Well, I can't say I fault him for that. It seems like the right trade for those of us accustomed to trouble.*

The Dark Elf, though, was a complete surprise. Usha

had never really had a reason to explore that part of the community and while she knew one was a member of the magical council, that particular individual walked with a limp and didn't seem particularly martial, she'd been told. This Drow—who was presumably the person who had blown the doors off the building—was a mystery, and not one she appreciated.

Then again, it's not like we're without surprises of our own. The girl and her people had put eyes on the place as soon as they discovered it would be their battleground, but the Atlantean team had already created secret accesses to avoid them. Using illusions, careful timing, and her watchers to watch their watchers, they'd placed traps in two of the buildings. She had hoped that Leblanc would follow her and fall for the one in there but should have realized the girl would stay with her pet. *No problem. Anything that winnows the numbers is good for us.*

She drew her sword and crouched behind a crate, ready to engage either the dwarf or the Drow the moment they were in range.

Tanyith led the way into the building that held the half-built ship. It appeared to be a large fishing vessel and was probably ninety feet long or more. Its deep hull was mostly complete, and a main level and upper cabin were each partially constructed. It was virtually impossible to see anything other than vague shapes in the darkness. The sound of sloshing came from the water that lapped below the suspended hulk.

"Let there be light," Wymarc quipped and threw the ball of lightning he held toward the ceiling high above. It cast shadows and served to dispel a little of the gloom and make the surrounding space slightly less ominous. The new illumination revealed an extensive work area that surrounded the vessel in a U-shape at ground level. This was littered with pieces of wood and metal and abandoned tools were scattered here and there. Unfortunately, it also showed a plethora of places the enemy duo might be hiding.

Tanyith pointed to himself and then to the right, and his partner nodded and moved in the other direction. He crept carefully around to the right and continued onto the part of the walk that went behind the boat. Danger accompanied each step as it seemed as if any piece of debris might slide underfoot if he stepped on it wrong. Worse, it was impossible to avoid all of it. His nerves were jumpy and even the noises he made caused him to flinch, in addition to the ambient sounds of the old structure.

If this were a horror movie, this is how the main character would go insane—from all the sounds and all the danger. And a jump scare would come at any moment. He shook his head at his nonsense and almost leapt out of his skin when a shadow shifted on the back wall. His first instinct was to discount it, but fortunately, his second one was smarter. He flung himself to the side to avoid the beam of shadow his foe launched at his face, landed with a clang of metal, and scrambled to his feet.

He cast shields through both daggers barely in time to catch the additional attacks that followed one after the other, as fast as any he had ever faced. While he hoped it meant they'd also be weaker than those that took longer, he somehow doubted it. The assault continued as the enemy stepped into view. In the darkness, he could barely make out the outline of the body enough to tell that it was the female. Everything else remained too vague except the sparkle in her eyes as she delivered more blasts of magic in a relentless rhythm.

Wymarc twisted toward the sound of crashing and realized he'd been played in time to summon a shield and block the burst of lightning that sought his heart. It made sense that they'd play off one another's moves, even if they weren't in proximity. The man emerged into the pale illumination cast by his ball of electricity above. *He looks younger than I thought outside. Maybe a little past his majority. And he is already smart enough to mess with our expectations by separating from his partner.*

"This is not your fight," the Jehenel patriarch offered. "You could leave along with your—uh, sister, I guess?"

The man's voice sounded young as well, filled with equal parts confidence and bravado. "But why would I do such a thing? It's not as if you're a threat to us."

"Do you know who I am?" He walked slowly back to change the angles. Right now, they were too close to the boat for the plan he had in mind.

His opponent scoffed, "Yes. I'm aware, *Patriarch*. But I don't care. Your kind has never had much use for those of us on the outskirts. Even if I wasn't paid well, I'd embrace the chance to kill you on general principles."

There goes that idea. He raised his hands and conjured a spear of force magic between them. The thread of lightning that would turn any touch into a shock made the object glow blue. Despite not being strictly physical, the wickedly sharp head would still stab through armor and flesh with ease.

His enemy raised his fists, each of which held a heavy cylinder. Large hooked blades snapped out at the top of each and made them look like ice-climbing axes. His foe waded in swinging, and with each slash, an arc of shadow magic burst out toward Wymarc. He blocked with his spinning spear and a single touch was enough to enable him to suck the power of the attack away. He continued to backpedal and darted hasty looks behind to ensure his footing.

The young patriarch didn't see the traitorous, trapped metal plates that erupted from beneath his feet and careened him back. He landed hard and heard the mocking laughter of his opponent—laughter that drew closer with each second.

Fyre swooped at the enemy handler but the man rolled easily out of the way of his grasping claws. *I had to try. The opportunity was there.* He'd gone into the maneuver knowing the probability of it being a trap was high, so when the rival Draksa barreled toward him from a blind spot, he was already diving and banking to evade the ambush.

He had a speed advantage on the other creature and

was nimbler when it came to changes in direction. But the defensive armor and the increased likelihood of damage from the other's bigger muscles if they went claw to claw at least evened the odds and maybe pushed them in his opponent's favor. *But I'm smarter. So there's that.*

Deliberately, he led his enemy away from Cali to prevent the other Draksa from making the same assault against her. So far, his foe hadn't revealed his breath weapon, but it would be stupid to think he lacked one. The Atlantean leader wouldn't have brought the Draksa and his partner along if they were limited. *Maybe he's waiting for the right moment or it's so close-range he hasn't had the chance yet. Either way, removing him before he can do it would be the best option.*

Quickly, he looped and made a much tighter turn than his pursuer would be able to emulate. The bigger creature slashed with his claws, and they raked his flesh to inflict a ragged gash. His gaze snapped down to see that the wicked talons were augmented with barbed sheaths above the natural point. He growled, eased behind the enemy Draksa, and discharged his frost breath in an attack he was sure would end the conflict.

When his foe suddenly banked and swooped twice as fast as his initial speed, Fyre realized he was in for more of a fight than he'd anticipated. A fierce burn began to radiate from his wound, a sign of the poison that must have coated the metal on his enemy's claws, and he thought for the first time that it might not end in his favor.

Zeb's path led him to a flight of stairs that climbed to the higher level of the warehouse. Nylotte had directed him upward when they'd entered and he complied without hesitation. He held Valerie in a low guard across his body, his left hand on the shaft and his right under the double-sided blade at the top. From that position, he could swing it, smash forward with it, or block in most directions. Knowing the caliber of their opponents, he advanced with more caution than he would have in his adventuring days. *Or maybe that's only age.*

The familiar rush of adrenaline was like a visit from a long-absent friend. His decision to step away from a life on the road seeking trouble wasn't because he disliked it. Quite the contrary, which was the problem. As his passion for fighting had grown, his concern about feeling that way had too. Finally, he'd hung it up before it could overwhelm him.

But still, *damn,* it felt good to knock the rust off and get back in the game for a round. The fight in the hospital had been barely an appetizer. This battle promised to be the main course. His growing enthusiasm didn't damage his awareness, though, which proved fortunate since the enemy second in command's ambush was almost perfect.

He'd expected her to be upstairs but her descent from the darkness of the rafters high above as he stepped onto the upper level was a surprise. Instinctively, he dove and rolled forward, took the brunt of the action on his shoulder, and sensed her weapon whipping through the air above him. He came out of it on his feet and immediately twisted to block. His rising ax caught the spear point inches from his face and lifted it over his head.

Zeb took a quick step in and stomped on Danna's foot, an attack the woman clearly hadn't anticipated to judge by her lack of defense. The distraction allowed him to shove a shoulder into her and knock her back, and he whipped the battle-ax in a horizontal chop at her stomach height. She stabbed the spear into the floor to intercept it, and slivers of ice broke away from the magical weapon. In a fluid motion, she swung it up, rotated it to drive his blade into the wooden planks on the other side, and levered the blunt bottom of her weapon at his face.

The dwarf scrambled away in alarm at the discovery that the bottom was also a blade but she managed a shallow cut along his forehead that immediately started to bleed into his eyes. The woman laughed as she spun away from his wild defensive swipe and twirled the spear over her head like she was some kind of helicopter. He slid his hand into the pouch at his waist and yanked out a magical bandage. When he slapped it against the wound, it stuck in place and began to heal the injury. It was faster to apply than fumbling with a healing potion but a little slower on the fix—perfect for such an insignificant injury.

Danna resumed her offensive again and she charged past him as she swung her weapon. He blocked cleanly and snagged her with his riposte, sliced through the black leather she wore, and cut into the flesh on her side. *No real damage. She twitched at exactly the right time. Quick little bunny.* He ceased his pursuit and dropped Valerie to summon his throwing axes in a single action. They twirled toward her as he bent to retrieve his battle-ax. She spun, lashed out with her spear, and knocked each of them off course barely enough to miss her. "You'll have to do better than that," she called.

He nodded. "All right, then. Since you asked so nicely." He surged forward with a battle cry. Her lips curled in a smile but he couldn't stop himself from stepping into the trap she'd set. His first reaction as the floor collapsed beneath him was that they must have been in the building for a while to prepare it. His second thought—which came as he broke through to the bottom level of the warehouse —was that they'd done a magnificent job of it. And his third thought, as he pounded into the concrete of the foundation hard enough to make him see stars was, *Hey, that's way too many big crates falling toward me.*

Cali's charge through her foe's flame attack had led to a series of exchanges, none of which were determinative. They'd cast magic at each other and she'd sipped from his power as he attacked and she blocked. Ironically, since his trident seemed able to do the same, she was probably simply reabsorbing her power. At another time, she might have found that funny. But now, with five of her friends in danger and the entire city's future on the line, all she wanted was to see him fall.

He paused occasionally to shoot magic into the air, presumably at Fyre. The Draksa were fighting veiled, so their presence was mainly a sensation—aside from all the cursing her partner was doing in her head. She felt his worry growing after a brief surge she'd interpreted as pain. *Are you okay, buddy?* she sent.

His response sounded much like a mental growl. *For the moment. Might need some help when this is over.*

She had to block her concern as her foe lunged with his trident and stabbed it low. When she blocked with Defender, he released the weapon with one hand and launched a lightning blast at her face. She caught it on her dagger, grounded the spell, and released the same attack at him. Again, it was inconclusive as he absorbed it with his trident.

Okay, if I can't get past the weapon, I'll have to overload it. She continued to fight but now only to maintain the status quo as she let the power build inside her. When it was ready, she released it in a sustained line of lightning that arced at her adversary. He raised his weapon horizontally to intercept it, and she poured more energy into the attack. *Let's see how much you can take, scumbag.*

Nylotte blocked the sounds of Zeb's progress up the stairs from her thoughts as she crept along the narrow lane that ran beside the wall. With no idea where her enemies might be hiding, she knew at least that her left side was probably safe—unless whoever had taken the ground floor could pass through solid objects. And since she hadn't learned how to do that yet, she doubted the enemy leaders had either. Like she'd told Cali, she didn't know everything but she did know considerably more than most.

The thought of Zeb's mention of knowing her past generated a smile. She liked the dwarf and respected that he'd done his homework exactly as she had. The two of them would have made quite a pair if they'd met in their respective adventuring days. Her mind snapped to the present as a scent carried to her, something out of place. She paused and focused on it but couldn't identify what it was. Still, she could tell where it probably came from— about ten feet ahead and from behind a crate.

"How about you come out and we do this like adults?" she called.

The Atlantean leader chuckled as she stepped into view. "Sure. Why not?" Usha wore leather armor with reinforced plates, lightweight but strong. The base layer was black, the dull metal a contrasting scarlet. She held a sword that looked exceptionally sharp and well-used.

Nylotte gestured with her chin. "Champion's gear?" Her adversary nodded. "Are those your house colors?"

The other woman laughed. "I have no house to speak of, so no. They are the colors of House Rivette, worn in honor of the Empress." The way she said it made the Dark Elf think tension existed between the Champion and her monarch.

"So, what's in all this for you?"

Usha shrugged. "I do what I'm told." A loud, sustained crashing issued from their right and the Drow flicked her sword in that direction, but no attack came. The other woman's voice called from above, "One down. Do you need a hand?"

"No, I think we're good here," her boss replied. "Go get the girl."

The Dark Elf shook her head. "We're far from good.

And any damage your ally did to my friend will be taken out of your hide."

The Champion of New Atlantis nodded. "Fair enough. Let's get to it, then." She raised her sword into a guard position and beckoned her forward.

Nylotte grinned. "Yes. Let's."

The Drow slipped into her version of a fighting stance, which kept her weight mostly on her back leg and allowed her to push off it quickly. She sent strength into her muscles automatically, an advantage of her extensive experience directing the magic where it needed to go without conscious thought. The result would be faster action and greater endurance, both of which she expected she would need against the Champion of New Atlantis.

She'd fought a wide variety of enemies in her day—monsters that looked like monsters, monsters that wore the guise of people, and everything between. The one common characteristic was that they all took advantage of folk they shouldn't have for food, power, wealth, or simply out of malicious intent.

The woman opposite her didn't fit those characteristics. Arguably, by following the orders of someone who sought to exert their will over others, she was culpable but overall, her interventions in New Orleans had been against other criminals. That earned her some credit in Nylotte's estimation.

Her adversary employed a martial approach that most would identify as a non-style. She moved in a direct line and chopped down with great vigor to meet her advance. The Drow flicked her sword tip enough to block the woman's weapon and almost lost her hold from the impact. Her eyes narrowed at the realization that her opponent might have increased her strength more than she could match. The Dark Elf changed her direct technique for a more fluid option that had much in common with Cali's preferred Aikido art but was far older and had been developed on Oriceran rather than Earth. Instead of meeting force with force, she focused on angles and redirection.

She found an opening and blasted her opponent with a burst of force that hurled her back. Usha turned her stumble into a somersault and came up with a bolt of lightning that streaked from her hand toward her adversary. The Drow raised a palm, grounded the magic, and pulled the power into her body to fuel her amplified muscles.

They entered an almost ritualistic exchange of assaults, trading sword cuts and spells as they felt out each other's capabilities. All battles against adequate opponents worked like that—the early dance to find a flaw followed by a fast attack to exploit it. Sometimes, it took longer to discover a vulnerability than one might prefer. She stabbed and the other woman parried and countered. When she blocked, Usha trapped her sword and tried a kick that she deflected with a blast of force powerful enough to knock it out of line and rob it of its power. Again and again, they clashed but repeatedly failed to discern the other's weakness.

Nylotte growled under her breath as frustration began to build. While on almost any other occasion she'd enjoy the challenge, a clock ticked in the back of her mind and counted off the passing minutes—minutes in which her allies might lose the war while she was busy winning the battle.

***

Fyre was, for all intents and purposes, on the run from the larger Draksa. When his opponent had revealed his true speed and strength, his reaction had been to gain some distance and hope he could blast the creature with frost. *At worst, it might slow him. At best, it might drop him. At double-best, it might drop him onto his handler's head.*

He didn't feel particularly charitable at the moment. The physical damage from the claw slash wasn't debilitating so much as annoying but the poison that seeped through his system slowed him more with each beat of his heart. It didn't feel like something that would kill him directly but if he lost focus and missed a dodge because of it, the result would be permanent.

On impulse, he spun, twisted to face his opponent, and belched a wide cone of frost at him. His pursuer couldn't avoid it and for a moment, Fyre's hopes sparked. Then his foe emerged from the flurry coated in ice that he broke off with each flap of his wings. He was only a few feet away. The smaller Draksa surged upward and dragged his claws against his foe's face in the same moment the creature breathed out and expelled acid across his lower half.

Fyre screeched in pain and anger and strength burst within him, a wash of power from Cali. He flipped and dove, coated his enemy in another wave of ice, followed it with another, and plunged after him as he plummeted and tried to escape the heavy cocoon. His rival landed hard and struggled to rise and he swooped past him once, twice, and again to slash and slice with his claws on each pass. The Draksa slumped, unconscious at least and hopefully more. He turned toward where he'd last seen Cali, ready to rush to her aid.

Cali whispered, "Thank you," to her sword, Defender, which had provided her with power for Fyre so she didn't have to break the stalemate with her opponent. They were still connected by an arc of electricity that flowed from her sword and dagger, followed a curve in the air between them, and terminated at his trident. The weapon was braced before him horizontally and glowed brighter with each passing moment.

A few seconds before, he'd begun to push back along the magic channel in an attempt to overwhelm her power with his. It was like a tug of war in reverse as each of them tried to shove more force, more magic, and more energy at the other. Her initial plea to her sword for energy had been for her use, but Fyre had needed it more at the moment of its arrival.

She sensed the Draksa turn to join their fight but

worried that anyone who interfered could fall victim to the combined power of both magics. *Go help Tanyith*, she sent. His emotions were tinged with reluctance but it felt like he had obeyed her command. She returned her attention to the man in front of her.

His face was rigid with fury, doubtless from the injury to his bonded partner. It was a positive sign for the enemy Draksa since if it had died, the man's mind probably would have snapped. That could have turned good or bad for her, depending on how he reacted. *I need to end this before his pet dies.* She forced words out of her throat loudly enough to be heard over their dueling magics. "Stop now. Go take care of your pet. We'll consider you off-limits."

He shook his head and a hint of madness flickered in his eyes. "Okay, then, I tried." She reached out to Fyre and pulled gently at his magic. He understood her need, opened the channel, and power flowed from him into her. She pushed it into the line connecting her to the handler, over-whelmed his resistance, and thrust it into the trident.

The magical weapon exploded. She shouted, *"Scield,"* in time for the charm's magical barrier to surround her and protect her from the magic-infused shards of metal. The handler fell with a scream and his damaged hands tried to cover his ravaged face. She waited to see what he would do, but when his only response was to rock on the ground in clear agony, she ceased drawing power from Fyre and let her shield fall. Quickly, she zip-tied his feet and wrists, retrieved a healing potion, and dribbled enough into his mouth to slow the blood flow to a trickle.

She would have helped him further, maybe, but the sight of Danna Cudon stalking toward her was suddenly much more important than the health of someone who had tried to kill her.

Tanyith's opponent stepped into a swath of illumination cast by Wymarc's hovering lightning globe. Her shiny black hair hung free around her, long enough to reach her waist. Weapons that resembled climbing axes were grasped in her fists, long shafts with a sharp extended hook jutting out near the end. She spun them idly as she advanced and on each rotation, another burst of magic emerged from the metal portion at the top.

It varied—bolts of shadow, fire, frost, electricity, and force were dispatched with no apparent pattern. The shields emanating from the points of his daggers were sufficient to intercept them, but keeping his defenses moving to the right places as she attacked along different vectors was a challenge. He had no thought of attacking, only of defending. Her pale, narrow face was expressionless and he might have been a bug for all she cared about him.

Briefly, he considered taunting her but didn't want to hear her voice. Part of him feared it would be as strange and ghostly as the rest of her. She seemed more to flow than to walk, and he knew he was overmatched. He was good but she had clearly spent much more time focused on combat than he had. But awaiting a rescue wasn't an option, as Wymarc would fight his own battle against the other one and might be even less equipped to do so than he was.

He needed to win. But how? The answer came to him in a burst of clarity, and he launched skyward on a burst of force toward the boat suspended over the center of the room. He landed on the half-finished deck and turned to see his foe arced in pursuit. From his higher vantage point, he saw Wymarc on his back below but he couldn't do anything to assist his partner. Instead, he ran through a doorway and headed down the stairs into the body of the ship.

<hr>

The ice ax thunked into the metal next to his head as Wymarc twisted to avoid it. Unfortunately, that left him exposed to the other one, which struck his leather armor on the shoulder. Most of its force was dissipated by the protective layer but it stabbed through nonetheless and buried itself in his flesh. He shouted the vilest curse he knew and kicked in fury to drive the top of his foot squarely between the other man's legs.

His assailant screamed and flung himself aside and away from him. In his flailing, he yanked the blade out, which did more damage than it had on the way in. The young patriarch rolled onto his stomach and pushed to his feet as tears welled in his eyes. His opponent looked like a ghost in the dim light with inky hair and pale skin. The man limped back, his gaze fixed on him.

Wymarc shook his head. "You should give up." He'd seen movement outside the building's open doorway and his enemy's retreat would carry him into that danger zone in seconds. "Drop your weapons and kneel on the ground.

I'll tie you up, but that's all. There's no need for you to die here." He released a blast of force at him as a warning, but it was blocked quickly. *Damn, he's recovering.* Before his advantage was lost, he surged at his opponent, who sensibly retreated.

His evasion took him directly into the claws of the Draksa who hurtled through the opening. Fyre lifted the man, carried him the scant distance to the boat, and flung him against it with all his built-up momentum. He pounded into the hull and fell senseless into the water.

"You go after him," Wymarc shouted. "Maybe he survived the collision. I think Tanyith's in the ship." He launched himself up toward the fishing vessel's deck.

The impact against the side of the craft resonated through the unfinished structure and dust filtered around him. Tanyith had reached the finished lower section, which was filled with debris and building materials. He'd discovered a place to hide behind a pile of wooden planks that would hopefully be invisible from the entrance. While he would have preferred to go deeper, the encroaching footsteps of his relentless shadow had been audible within moments after he'd entered the ship's main cabin area above.

The light shone through gaps in the partial deck above him. He relied on ears more than eyes because he was tucked half under the pieces of wood and could only see out at a particular angle, one that didn't show the entry. The creak of leather sounded over the other noises, though, discordant enough to be identifiable. He waited and watched, his muscles tensed for the moment his enemy would step into view.

The blast lifted him and hurled him deeper into the ship, along with a shower of flaming wooden splinters. He wound himself in a force shield to absorb the impact and rolled to his feet. By the time he reoriented, the woman had almost reached him and it became very clear that her former dispassion had been replaced by anger. He caught her ax strikes on his daggers and snapped a kick at her knee. She twisted enough to take it on the side where it couldn't do much damage and retaliated with the thunk of an ax handle against his skull.

He shook his head to clear the stars from his vision and intercepted her next two attacks, one physical and one magical. Absently, he took note of the fact that the wooden portions of the ship were now on fire, including the deck he stood on. Above him was open air and the Draksa flashed through it and uttered a screech as he passed. It was enough to distract the woman for an instant, and that was all he needed.

Tanyith launched a double blast of force magic through his daggers, both aimed directly at her solar plexus. The impact stole her breath and she fell, and it was only the work of a minute to secure her. Fyre swooped and iced the flames as Wymarc appeared above and yelled, "Let's go."

No second invitation was needed and he launched himself out of the boat after the young patriarch to find Cali.

CHAPTER ELEVEN

Zeb waited until he was sure the collapse was finished and delayed for a minute more before he took action beyond the hasty force barrier he'd conjured a foot above his face. It wasn't the first time he'd fallen into a pit and although the particular shield he'd summoned under him as he fell didn't absorb all the impact, it had diminished the familiar ringing in his ears somewhat. That particular defense was attuned to deal with pointy objects more than sudden stops.

If this had been my trap, there would have been spikes. If I felt nasty, poisoned spikes.

He groaned at the thought. *And that's exactly why I gave up the adventurer game. There is too much opportunity for viciousness.* Even though the stack of fallen items above him was significantly heavy, it posed no danger to him. With the magic stored in Valerie—power he had transferred to the weapon in small drips and drops over time—he could maintain the current situation until he passed out from boredom.

Fortunately, a better option existed that he also had enough power for. He poured magic into the shield and raised it, which caused the boxes blocking him to recede. When they were above the first floor, he got his feet beneath him and used force magic to assist in a jump that carried him up and through the opening. As he landed, the boxes plummeted behind him in a satisfying cacophony. Sounds of nearby combat echoed over the continued bells in his ears, and he dashed toward it.

He discovered Nylotte in a furious battle with the enemy leader. The two moved faster than he'd ever seen anyone fight, even those he'd run with in the past who regularly amped themselves with magic. Swords clashed against each other, kicks and punches were thrown and blocked, and magical assaults were discharged and absorbed. Their dance was remarkable, and a large part of him wanted to do nothing more than watch.

But it was also a distraction from their purpose there, which was to make the damned Atlanteans quit their nonsense. Watching wasn't an option. He clambered onto a crate and shouted, "Hey, knock it off, you two." They disengaged with the same rapidity with which they'd fought and turned to look at him. He grinned. "You're done, Usha. Put your weapons down and call it a day."

She shook her head. "I still have one card to play." Her sword suddenly glowed red and orange and he flinched reflexively while Nylotte backed away. The Atlantean leader carved through the metal wall of the building as if it were paper and rocketed through the opening.

The Drow looked at him with respect in her eyes. "She is a being to be reckoned with."

He hopped down to follow said being and broke into a run. "And we have to stop her from reaching Cali."

Danna had wanted to find the girl engaged with an opponent so she could sweep in and do what needed to be done without becoming involved in a drawn-out fight. Sadly, the sight of the bound Draksa handler told the tale of the girl's victory in yet another conflict. *But a fight isn't the battle.* Usha was the only ally she cared about, and she hoped the other woman was safe. She pushed that worry out of her mind since it was apparently up to her to end the game against the young matriarch.

She ran toward the center of the dock and a place marked by a discolored panel. As expected, the girl tracked her and ran along a diagonal that would intersect her path about twenty feet past her goal. By the time she reached the trigger, Leblanc was within the effective range, so she stamped hard and cast the magic.

Depressing the block made the magical circle's path complete, and the spell created a barrier that encircled the position, fifty feet in diameter with a domed top. It would prevent others from joining their battle and would last until she dispelled it or died. Ozahl had helped her prepare it and watched from somewhere close, ready to rescue her if things went awry. His power fueled the shield. Hers was needed for more imminent concerns.

The girl slowed, stopped, and turned to face her. "What's all this, then?"

Her fake British accent made Danna laugh. "I thought we could have a private word."

"Only a word?"

She shrugged. "Okay, more than a word."

Caliste shook her head. "Listen. None of your people are around, which means they've probably lost. Why don't you give up? Is New Orleans worth dying for?"

Danna sighed. "No, New Orleans isn't. But other things are." The sight of Usha running into view distracted her. The look on her friend's face was pained as the shielded fight with the girl was the last resort. At this point, unless they killed Leblanc, they had lost the city. The Champion of New Atlantis had become a non-factor in her own fate, which the woman would not handle well. Her second in command tilted her head in the direction of the road. Her friend nodded and ran to safety since she no longer had the ability to change the outcome.

"How about the lives of those we've captured, rather than killing them?" the girl asked. "If you surrender now, they live."

She laughed. "Please, Matriarch. We both know you won't kill them, so why pretend any different? No, this is it. You and me for the prize of the city."

A frustration equal to Usha's had settled on Caliste's face. "Why? Why do all this?" She gestured around them. "If it was going to come down to this, why risk all those people?"

"That's a good question." *It is, actually.* "I guess the best answer is because that's how it's done in New Atlantis—how it's always been done. You're the leader of a noble house. You know how tradition works down there."

"But it doesn't have to be like this."

Danna shrugged. "Maybe over time, you or other matriarchs or patriarchs can make a change and start some new traditions. But for now, this is what we have."

Her opponent's face changed and hardened as she accepted the inevitability of their battle. "I suppose incapacitation won't do?"

"Not on my part."

She nodded. "Okay, wench. Bring it."

The Atlantean second in command clearly couldn't be reasoned with. She was as combative and martial as Cali had ever seen her. Her slicked-back hair left her face looking even more angular and severe than usual. The suits that normally only hinted at the form beneath had hidden her muscular build, which was obvious in her fitted black leather armor. It covered her from neck to toe and looked rather similar to what Nylotte wore, and it would doubtless include both magical and physical protection as well.

She had no idea what was at work in the other woman's mind. With her allies defeated or run off, there seemed to be little value in continuing the fight. Her connection with Fyre was still present but muted through the shield, which made it her least reliable backup plan. She had more power in the sword, two energy draughts, and two and a half healing potions. Plus a few extra toys that she'd prefer to hold in reserve in case the Malniets had eyes on this battle. If the situations were reversed, she would have paid good money for a preview of her prospective opponents' abilities.

The shield that surrounded them was an unexpected twist, but she couldn't be overly unhappy about it. At least now, her allies were safe—assuming they'd won their individual battles. She reached into Defender to initiate the connection that would allow her to pull magic and sensed the presences of those who had put their essences into the sword. This time, there were far more than only the two she had previously faced, all willing to support her needs.

Danna tapped the thumb sides of her fists together and drew them apart slowly. Her ice spear formed and extended to a blade at both ends. These had cutting surfaces at four angles that tapered into a point. Cali had seen the weapon before and Tanyith had reported that it was doubly pointy. Facing it now, she judged he had significantly understated the situation. She summoned her fighting stick to her left hand and held Defender at the ready in her right.

Her enemy gave her a final nod, darted in, and led with the point of her spear. Cali brought her sword around to block from the outside in, twirled away from the thrusting point, and whipped her stick in a backhand slash, her spine against the icy staff. A burst of force shoved her forward when she touched the weapon, and she staggered several feet before she made a quick shuffle to her right and whirled to face her foe.

The action wasn't a second too soon. Her sword deflected the spear point enough out of line that it didn't pierce her uniform shoulder but scraped up and over it instead. Danna followed with a front kick that she blocked automatically with a raised foot. She threw her stick at the other woman, who jerked her head to the side to avoid it. With a slight grin, she recalled it and the returning weapon smacked Danna in the back of the head. The blow lacked power but was enough to break her concentration.

Cali raced forward and chopped down with her sword. Her foe blocked it with a twirl of the staff and swished the bottom at her skull. She dropped under it and turned the dodge into a leg sweep, but the Atlantean leapt over it and backpedaled out of range.

She rose warily, ready for the next attack. Danna provided it an instant later when she circled left and thrust repeatedly with the spear to force her to focus on block after block. As soon as a pattern was created, the other woman broke it, stabbed once, and immediately repeated the thrust. Cali managed an X-block to stop the weapon, but the cascade of lightning that surged out of the tip savaged her. She jerked and twitched as she backpedaled and tried to absorb the magic like Nylotte had taught her.

Mostly, she failed and focused instead on not toppling as her enemy flowed into another assault. She sent her will into the sword in search of assistance, and Defender replied. The electricity was sucked into the blade, which glowed bright blue after the influx. She slashed it upward with a shout of relief and it met the ice spear a foot from her nose. Danna's weapon shattered and shrapnel scattered everywhere, exactly as the trident had done before. This time, she couldn't say the word to activate her shield fast enough and collapsed with shards of metal in her face. She struggled to breathe and fumbled at her thigh pouch for her healing potion.

Fyre sent her strength, which was all that enabled her to remain conscious. Another hand caught hers before it could find the potion she needed to survive. She threw her other fist up in a weak punch and her opponent caught it as she crouched over her stomach. Danna stared into her eyes from above. She had also been injured, her face sliced in a dozen places that welled blood. She shook her head.

"You're a worthy foe, Caliste Leblanc. I can't possibly end your story now if only because there's a tiny chance your allies will catch me before I can escape. Give me your word that you'll let me go and you get to live."

Cali nodded and tried to speak but couldn't. Her adversary returned the nod. "Close enough." She removed the healing flask from the girl's thigh pouch and dribbled a few drops into her mouth, then wrapped her hand around it so she could continue without her help. She stood and shouted, "You heard?"

When the girl turned her head, Zeb held his battle-ax like he intended to destroy the world with it but nodded. "We heard. Get out." After a shimmer of magic and a rustle of movement, Fyre was on one side of her and Zeb on the other. The dwarf helped her swallow more potion and sit. After the wave of weirdness that always accompanied rapid healing had faded, she started to laugh.

Nylotte's voice was long-suffering. "What are you laughing at now, Caliste?"

The sound made her laugh harder. "Oh, nothing. Only that we won. The Atlanteans lost. And I learned how to ask the sword for what I need and have it listen. The Malniets don't stand a chance."

CHAPTER TWELVE

S henni scowled at Gwyn as the seneschal extended the formal robe that was unquestionably the appropriate choice given the day's tasks. "Is that necessary?"

The other woman shook her head with a soft sigh. "Yes, Empress, you know it is." This was doubtless a tone she had used with her children in the past and it held traces of love and exasperation.

As the oldest child and heir of House Rivette, her parents had been good to her. She'd grown up in relative luxury but with a practical edge. Her family knew their place in the hierarchy of the Nine wasn't assured and that as one of the smaller houses, they would have to fight for prominence again and again. *Well, I certainly exceeded their expectations.*

With a sigh in response, the Empress extended her arms so her two valets could put her in the garment. She'd already endured the ministrations of hair and makeup specialists and now, only one thing remained to do. When she nodded at Gwyn, the other woman moved to the locked cabinet in her dressing room. It required spells and keys to permit entry and once opened, revealed her royal accessories.

The seneschal donned the ceremonial leather gloves hanging on the door as only the monarch was permitted to touch the objects with bare skin. She handed them to her one by one. First, the necklace, which was gold adorned with rubies and sapphires that sparkled in red and blue with the stylized shark that denoted House Rivette hanging as a pendant. Second came the crown, which was made of a simple gold circlet with diamonds all around. Finally, the scepter was a long thin tube with a sphere on the top made of gold and adorned with pearls.

Once that process was complete, it was time to move. Gwyn opened the main doors and preceded her into the outer room and into the hall, where she motioned for a squad of guards to move ahead of them. Another two fell into place behind her as she strode past, and two more took position outside the entrance to her private chambers to ensure no one accessed them while she was away.

The walk to the throne room was not lengthy, although it seemed that way, burdened as she was with both the physical and emotional weights of the monarchy. She banished the latter in cadence with each step and transformed from Shenni, who was allowed to feel, into the Empress of New Atlantis, who most definitely was not. By the time they reached the throne room and she walked the scarlet carpet, her face was impassive and fully controlled. A small throng of people bowed on each side as she strode through the center. At the top of the stairs, she deposited the scepter into its holder, turned, and took her place on the oversized throne.

She sent a telepathic message to Gwyn, and the woman nodded and gestured at the doors, which had closed behind them. The attendants pulled them inward again to reveal the matriarch of House Cormier and the patriarch of House Malniet standing beside one another. She smiled at them with parental condescension. They strode forward slowly, their chins high, and basked in the attention from the courtiers to either side who had been brought there at this moment for that specific purpose.

The event was, quite literally, the least Shenni could do. She had no time for anything more with the power arrangement in her city in flux. Nor did she have the will to celebrate the union any more publicly than this. Styrris hadn't earned it. Once he'd done his part and rid them of House Leblanc, then and only then would she consider hosting the celebration she'd promised him. He'd bucked at the restriction but in the end, he was only one of nine and she was the monarch.

The bride was dressed in Cormier dark-green trimmed with white. Her gown was long and flowing but not so much as to require attendants. That, too, would have to wait for the more public version of the ceremony. Styrris, always elegant, had simply chosen one of his more formal uniforms—shining shoes below black trousers and jacket, a black shirt buttoned to the neck, and a golden jeweled pin at the throat that displayed the wicked hook that represented House Malniet. He strode stiffly, his eyes not on his bride but only on his ruler.

As it should be at this particular moment. His attempt to

kill the girl had gone awry, which irritated Shenni. That failure had necessitated that the battle on the surface take place. Although Usha had not yet reported the results of the contest from two nights before, the other informants scattered throughout the gang all told the same tale. Leblanc, against all odds, had won again. If the Empress wished to claim New Orleans for herself, she would have to send an entirely different group to begin rebuilding from the ground up according to the rules.

But once Leblanc falls, perhaps the votes will be right to change those rules. And if not, well, houses are always rising and falling, are they not? Her lips twisted into a small smile as the couple reached the base of the dais, and if the crowd misinterpreted it as being directed at the bride and groom, so much the better. She rose to begin the ceremony.

An hour later, she glided into her office through the rear door in far more comfortable clothes—a simple but elegant suit—and nodded at the newlyweds seated on the opposite side of the large desk. She greeted them as she took her seat. "Less formally but no less genuinely, congratulations. It is always a cause for celebration when the head of one of the nine houses weds and all the more so when two of them do."

Brielle inclined her head stiffly. Her figure was even thinner than her husband's, which was saying something. Her mousey brown hair was unimpressive, as was the unhappy expression she wore. Gwyn had discovered that it was indeed a family member further down the Cormier line who had made the deal that handed the woman to Styrris. They would not ascend to lead the house but had a significant influence on the person who would, which worked in the Malniets' favor.

Plus, having such a young bride will draw envy from people stupid enough to care about such things.

Styrris's posture—leaning back in his chair with his fingers steepled—was one step short of disrespectful. To be fair, that was to be expected. She'd made a deal with him and would continue to string him along until he delivered on his promises. This stopgap solution of a non-public wedding was ostensibly a partial payment of her debt but was more for her purposes. Now, Cormier would have a claim on Malniet if the house fell. It would muddy the waters, and anything that confused the nine was to her benefit. On the other hand, the new connection would also distract Malniet. Another win.

He sighed. "Yes, congratulations indeed. And thank you for delivering on at least one of your commitments, Empress." His tone took a step over the line separating respect from disrespect, but she decided to let it pass. Unknown to him—or anyone other than her family and Gwyn—the guards stationed at the door were unlike any who had stood in that position before. Today, they were under the mental control of one of her relatives, who was behind the false wall with the archers. They would kill without a thought and even the possibility of thought at her word. Although the Leblanc girl had created some disruption in her family's research, they had quickly recovered what was lost.

She pressed her lips together in a thin smile. "You're

welcome, of course, Patriarch. But my keen sensibilities tell me you are still dissatisfied." She chuckled with him as he laughed and leaned forward.

"True, Empress. I recall talk of a celebration and a dowry of some kind. Unless it's a surprise party, it appears to be absent. I also don't see a pile of gems in your office."

Shenni flicked her gaze to Brielle Cormier. The woman looked ill as if the stress of the moment was too much for her to take. *Perhaps the relative who sold her to this walking corpse did the right thing for the house. She doesn't have the backbone to lead if this bothers her.* Then, she reconsidered. *Or maybe it's the wedding night that makes her seem like she's about to collapse.* She shuddered. *It would do that to me too.* She returned her gaze to Styrris and kept her face carefully neutral. "You have not yet fulfilled the terms of our agreement, Patriarch. Surely you don't imagine I would pay in advance?"

He shrugged. "I could hope."

"And you can keep on hoping but that won't make it any more likely. Deliver what you've promised and you will have what you seek, but not an instant before. Is that completely clear? I feel like we've had this conversation twice now. Bringing it up a third time wouldn't be good for anyone involved."

Styrris nodded with a distinct lack of concern. "Very well, Empress. As you say."

She leaned back with a nod and gestured to Gwyn, who stood against the back wall. The seneschal bustled forward with a tray of drinks already poured—dark rum for each of them—and offered the guests their choice of glass. Shenni took the remaining one and drank from it, proving that she wasn't attempting to poison her visitors. *There are ways, of course. An antidote cleverly applied as the cup is handed to me. Or an immunity built up over time.* But now was not the moment to throw away the strategic advantage the conflict between Leblanc and Malniet provided.

"So, will you agree to the girl's terms?" she asked. "A single battle to finish it? It seems as if that suits your purposes best, as well."

He nodded. "I intend to. Originally, I had planned to have four champions to ensure killing her and her top supporters. However, one is recently unavailable, so it will be three on three."

Shenni raised an amused eyebrow. "You could always step in, Styrris. I've heard you're quite good with a sword."

The patriarch straightened a little at the false compliment. "Quite good, perhaps, Empress, but I have no interest in combat with the girl and her lizard. No, I have people for that—people far better than me at dealing death face-to-face."

Her smile inched a little wider. *Patriarch, how bold. I do believe that was a threat.* She turned to Brielle. "I wish you the most pleasurable of wedding nights, Matriarch Cormier. I am sure Styrris will not disappoint." She stood and her guests rose and bowed slightly before they turned and were led out by two guards who entered from the hall.

When the door had closed, Shenni sat again and Gwyn took the seat across from her. The seneschal said, "I don't envy her."

She waved a dismissive hand. "She made her bed. Or her family made it for her. If she's smart, she'll kill him as soon as she can. A bold move at this time of uncertainty could cause real trouble for his House. She could ally with Leblanc."

Her companion snorted. "She strikes me as prey rather than predator, Empress."

Shenni lifted the glass to her lips, drained it, and set the empty crystal vessel gently on the desk. "Prey can be quite dangerous when cornered. I think Patriarch Malniet would be wise to remember that where his new bride is concerned—as well as where his enemy is concerned."

"Do you think Leblanc is prey?"

"I think Styrris is arrogant and that he will think so."

The older woman sighed. "I have to agree. You shouldn't have offered him rum. He can't afford the loss of the brain cells."

She laughed. "If he survives what is to come, he could be a useful tool. If not, you may poison him and we'll move on to the next."

Gwyn lifted Brielle's glass which was still full and raised it in a toast to her monarch before she drained it. "Now that, my Empress, is a plan I can believe in."

CHAPTER THIRTEEN

Cali plopped on the chair beside Emalia at the large wooden table in the Leblanc mansion's kitchen. She didn't speak and simply ran her hand along the wood grain and made noises of appreciation. Fyre bumped her seat as he crawled under it to take his hundred and seventy-fifth nap of the day—*probably, although I may have lost count somewhere in the middle of the afternoon.* Finally, the other woman's restraint snapped.

She slammed the book she was reading onto the table and growled her annoyance. "What do you want, Caliste?" Someone who didn't know her well might even conclude she was serious.

The girl broke into laughter and her great-aunt joined her. Fyre snorted and radiated amusement across the channel that connected them. "There's the great-aunt I adore." She stood and walked a few feet to the cooler, opened it, and retrieved a Coke she'd imported from the tavern. "Do you want anything?"

"No thanks. I'd be up all night if I had caffeine."

"I could make you tea."

"Invel will make me tea."

Cali sat beside the older woman with a knowing grin. "Oh, Invel will take care of you, will he?" The romance that had begun on the surface had blossomed under the waves, and she was entirely glad for it. Her great-aunt had always been a treasure, and it was good to see her happy and no longer quite so solitary.

"Shut it, you," Emalia said, but her face and eyes both showed her pleasure at the notion.

"So, what have you found out, Leblanc spymaster woman?"

The older woman gestured toward the three stacked listening devices that had been relocated from the table to a shelf. "Well, nothing interesting is going on with House Terriau other than the younger generation plotting their moves for when the matriarch has shuffled off this lifetime."

"They're not planning to hasten that, are they? Because I like Icille Terriau a lot."

Her aunt nodded. "Me too. No, they're mainly complaining that since I visited, the matriarch is even more annoying than she was before."

She laughed. "So you'll keep visiting, right?"

"Oh, hell yes." Emalia shook her head. "I tell you, young people today—"

Cali interrupted her great aunt with a raised hand. "Shush. What about from the palace?"

"That one's not useful anymore. The last thing I heard was scraping and muttering, and after listening to it twenty times or so, Invel and I agree. It was the sound of a chair being moved into storage."

She sighed. "And after all your effort to sneak it in there. That sucks."

The woman shrugged. "Win some, lose some. The grapevine says Styrris and Brielle got hitched earlier today. The poor girl." She shook her head. "That man is nauseating."

"I feel the same. But she chose to marry him, right?"

"Or the choice was made for her. Either way, I wouldn't wish that fate on an enemy."

Cali took a long sip of her Coke. Once things settled, finding a supply chain to provide her with glass bottles of the beverage would be one of her top priorities. "And speaking of enemies, what do you hear from the old man himself?"

"Mainly an endless litany of insults and chastisements for his servants and his family. But there was some useful news in there as well. Apparently, a couple of people he was counting on to fight on his behalf have gone missing."

The girl smiled, then frowned. "Wait. While anything that makes Styrris's life a little less enjoyable is a-okay in my book, we're not eliminating his potentials while he's not looking, are we?"

Emalia shook her head. "None of us here in the house is. And if you aren't, I guess it could be a coincidence."

She tapped the table with a fingernail. "That's an interesting coincidence. By which I mean probably not a coincidence at all. I'd like to know what's going on there."

"I'll talk to some people and see what I can find out."

"Starting with Icille?"

Her great aunt laughed. "Of course. She's a treasure trove of gossip."

Not entirely enthusiastically, Cali had agreed to meet Wymarc for dinner again, solely because she felt she owed him. His appearance to fight alongside her team in the battle against the Atlanteans in New Orleans had been part of what had enabled her to win. That deserved something, at least, even though he'd said no reward was required.

She didn't like owing people so when he'd asked, she'd accepted, mostly out of a sense of obligation. The rest of the reason was that she genuinely enjoyed his company and friends were hard to come by. Especially friends who were also the leaders of a noble house. *You can't have too many of those.*

The venue was somewhere she hadn't been before, and the menu was filled with unfamiliar dishes. He guided her to a selection of fish that turned out to be wonderful. They talked over the meal about things both unimportant and very important, including the political climate in New Atlantis and the potential fallout from the fight on the surface.

"So, how do you think the loss upstairs affects Empress Shenni?" she asked,

Wymarc paused in mid-bite, set his fork down, and patted his lips with a white napkin. It stood out dramatically against the dark shirt he wore. She'd been surprised when he'd arrived all in black. Her Johnny Cash joke flew right past him, which was understandable but still depressing.

"Well, since that was her plan," he replied, "it certainly doesn't make her look good. At best, she's only lost face so far. If she can install a new group of people and accomplish what she set out to do, this minor glitch will probably be forgotten."

Cali frowned. "They can't do that. I won."

He shook his head. "The particular individuals you fought are the ones who challenged you. New people, new challenge."

She groaned. "So the whole thing was for nothing?"

"Never that. You accomplished some very important things. First, your city is far more ready to deal with the situation if it happens again. That will give Shenni at least a moment's pause since she doesn't want to look stupid a second time. Next, that was the New Atlantis Champion you defeated. Anyone who takes over will be less capable by definition. Finally, the other magicals in the city won't forget what happened. They'll be much quicker off the bat from here on out." He picked his fork up again. "No, your win comes with good things even though not with every good thing you might have wanted."

"Okay. I can work with that. We'll focus on getting defenses in place so we're ready to go if she tries again."

He chuckled, said, "That's the spirit," and finished the red wine in his glass. She poured him another half-portion. "Thanks. So, when will you hear from Styrris, do you think?"

"Emalia tells me she assumes he'll have something to say tomorrow. He got married today. Did you know that?"

Wymarc nodded. "I did. That word traveled like wild-fire. It's a big deal, marriage between the houses."

"I assume it doesn't happen often because no one wants to give up their power to join with another house?"

"You nailed it in one."

Cali sipped the wine in her glass, then asked, "So why do you think she did it?"

He shrugged. "Almost certainly, she was pressured to. By the Malniets or people in her family, or maybe even the Empress herself. There's no way I can see anyone agreeing to marry him, much less someone as young as Brielle Cormier."

"That's Emalia's take on it, too."

"She's a smart woman. I'm not sure how you missed out on that genetic bonus."

She laughed and made a rude gesture at him. "Why did I agree to have dinner with you again?"

"Because I'm never boring."

"That's…very fair." She laughed because he'd earned the point. "Good deal." The conversation moved on to other topics and by the time they left, she realized that she was truly enjoying herself. Her mind had even let its multitude of worries go for a while to allow it to happen, which was impressive in and of itself.

The sight of six figures blocking their path as they turned toward the palace was an unwelcome discovery. They were in pairs, two in the front, the next two on the right, and those in the back on the left. Of those closest, one was clearly older—a woman who, in this light, resembled Styrris but was a couple of decades or so less ancient. She spoke harshly. "Hello, Leblanc."

Wymarc sighed and twisted to face Cali. "Seriously? Before you ask, no, this isn't me. Can't you have one pleasant night out without someone trying to kill you, and by extension, me?" He didn't give her time to answer but turned to the woman who had spoken. "This is the part where you tell me I can leave as long as I don't get involved, right?"

Their apparent enemy smiled and shook her head. "I'm afraid not, Patriarch. The orders are for both of you. You've chosen your side and as usual, your decision is unwise."

He frowned. "That's not very polite."

She rolled her eyes and looked at his companion. "Any last words, Matriarch?"

Cali sent a mental message to Fyre, who was flying invisibly overhead, and readied herself to attack. Before she could open her mouth to reply, Wymarc intervened. "Now would be good," he said.

With quick and brutal efficiency, the four in the back swarmed over the two in the front, attacked them before they had time to even register the apparent betrayal, and took advantage of their defenselessness. In moments, the two were on their knees with their hands behind their heads, weaponless and angry.

She turned to him. "Do you care to explain?"

He shrugged. "It was inevitable that Styrris would send someone to assassinate you. I reached out to my mercenary friends who, generally speaking, view the Malniets as a family of scumbags. I offered to double whatever payment they got for intervening at my request. Or, if I wasn't with you, they would have acted on their own judgment."

Cali shook her head. "Why?"

"I would think that would be obvious. I wronged you and I'm determined to make it right."

"We're even after this, I think."

The young man chuckled. "On the day that we manage to go out to dinner without getting attacked, I'll consider the debt paid."

"Okay, deal." She laughed before she looked at the captives with a frown. "What should we do with those two?"

"They're minor players in the house but it wouldn't do to have them telling tales. The dungeons below the Jehenel mansion are reasonably clean and well kept. They can stay there for a while until your disagreement with Malniet is resolved."

"It'd be easier to kill them," one of the mercenaries who had turned on the others observed. "It would send a message, too."

"Easier, sure, but wasteful," Wymarc replied. "Today's enemy is tomorrow's ally." He gestured at the two prisoners. "Get them to my place. I'll meet you there."

He'd make a good boyfriend, Fyre sent into her mind.

She returned, *Shut up you,* but was secretly pleased that the Draksa had decided to forgive the patriarch for his initial foolishness. *As if I have time for a relationship, anyway.*

Her partner laughed. *As if you could get one if you did.*

Cali shook her head. *You're lucky I need you, scale-face, or it'd be curtains for you. Curtains, I say.* His laughter echoed in her ears as she turned to Wymarc. "So, how about we try this whole escorting-me-home thing again?"

CHAPTER FOURTEEN

A messenger from Malniet had arrived and been rebuffed by Emalia, who acted as Cali's representative. If Styrris wouldn't arrive himself, she couldn't afford the loss of face to speak to his underling. *Which is stupid, wasteful, and a whole horde of other adjectives.* Instead, the girl stayed in the kitchen, drinking hot chocolate and throwing marshmallows at Fyre.

The Draksa snatched them in mid-air with quick snaps of his snout. His goal was to allow none to hit the floor. Her goal was to bean him between the eyes. She hadn't managed it yet but was confident that over a long enough timeline, he'd let his guard down. *And this nonsense with the messenger leaves me with nothing but time.*

She felt less relieved about the resolution of the situation with the Atlantean gang than she'd expected to. While it was an issue off her plate, it wasn't the greatest one. She still had to defeat the Malniets to get the answer she needed—the solution to how to keep her brother alive. Having the sword was useless without that additional knowledge unless she wanted to release him from his magical protections only to watch him fade away.

And double-damned Styrris Malniet is delaying and delaying. Coward. It's not like he'll even show up and fight himself. She would never get that lucky. No, the patriarch of the enemy house would secure the best fighters available and send them against her and her friends. Her greatest fear was that he'd want big numbers on each side. His wealth and influence were greater than hers and that might leave her at a disadvantage. Emalia was on that, as well, rounding up what funds they could easily put their hands on and researching allies for rent in New Atlantis.

Both Wymarc and Tanyith had suggested that perhaps cutting the head off the enemy outside the rules would be the better choice, and she'd seriously considered following their advice. But the only way to ensure that she got what she wanted was to defeat them in the ritual, which would compel them to release the knowledge to her. Any other route gave them an out to deny her demand.

When the third knock on the door came, Fyre twisted his head and she managed to hit her target. "Yes!" she crowed. "Cali wins! Cali wins!" He turned to look at her with annoyance and discharged a small fog of frost breath at her. She spun out of her chair, laughing, and pointed a finger at him. "Hey. Play fair. It's not my fault you're so easily distracted."

"You have to sleep sometime. It'll be a cold, frosty night for you." His playful growl always made her happy.

Emalia stepped into the kitchen. "The meeting is set." They both turned to face her. "Two hours. On the palace grounds, equally between the houses."

She sighed. "So symbolic. So dramatic. Idiot." She shook her head and corrected herself quickly. "Styrris. Not you."

Her great-aunt chuckled. "I know, sweetheart. He'll almost certainly have people out watching the area already. You should do the same."

"Invel and Fyre?"

"Unless there are more folks hanging around here who I'm unaware of. I don't think Scoppic wants to be disturbed. He's lost in a history of Oriceran that dates before any of the others we've found."

Cali grinned. "Well, we wouldn't want to interrupt him, then. Jenkins," she asked the air, "you're bound to the house, right?"

The disembodied majordomo replied, "To the grounds, Matriarch Caliste. Although I am strongest within the mansion."

"Why?"

He laughed. "That is beyond my knowledge, Matriarch. You would have to ask your ancestors."

"Fair enough. So, you and Emalia can hold down the fort here in case they try something, Invel and Fyre will keep an eye out before, during, and after, and I'll meet Styrris and see what he has to say." She headed to the stairs to change and muttered, "Why do I always wind up with the worst jobs?"

Her dressing room was mostly a disaster as she had a tendency to try things on and toss them aside rather than putting them back where they belonged. Since her visits to New Atlantis were invariably on the run, she hadn't yet managed the second part of the cycle where she cleaned the chamber. Emalia would have done it for her—or hired someone to—but she refused. This was her special place and she didn't want anyone messing with it.

Cali pawed through the outfits still hanging in the tall wooden wardrobe and sighed at her failure to discover anything she liked. Next was the dresser, created from the same unfamiliar wood as the larger piece of furniture. Again, nothing appealed to her. She sifted through the stacks of previously discarded clothes on the room's large comfortable chairs and the footrests that went with them, those on the hook on the back of the door and the door handle, and even some suspended on the rod that held the curtains covering the wide window.

Finally, she found some things she could work with. Heavy black denim jeans that were a little baggy plus a pair of matching work boots would do for the bottom layer. The footwear was high enough to hide the sheaths for throwing knives inside, so she added them. *Not that I'm particularly good at it but it's always better to have more options than less, right?* Next up was a dress in black and red that fit her tightly but stretched when she needed to move. It reached her hands with a piece that went between her fingers to keep it properly positioned. She slid her magic bracelets over it.

Finally, a stylish belt of silver links finished the outfit. She slipped her daggers into sheaths on each side as weapons hadn't been specifically prohibited. Ostensibly, it was for display purposes only, but she had little doubt that Styrris would be equally well-armed, either with physical blades or magical ones. She checked the look in the mirror, pulled her hair out of its ponytail and shook it free, and decided it was good enough for her meeting with the desiccated leader of her rival house.

Fyre, flying high above the palace grounds, spoke into her mind. *He's left his mansion.*

Cali nodded and stepped out the door, which Emalia closed behind her. She tried to imagine what Styrris's walking pace would be and slowed hers by half to match it. *It wouldn't do to be the first one there—or the last one. No, we have to arrive together for some bizarre and stupid reason.*

Fyre laughed. *Thinking loud again. And it is bizarre and stupid. Draksa would never do something like that.*

She chuckled. *No, you'd flap around playing chase and demonstrating your lack of maturity."*

You're one to talk.

Yeah, yeah. She was too tense to continue the conversation and focused on making her way to the appointed place at the appointed time. Her partner kept her updated on her enemy's progress, and she changed her speed as needed. When she stepped onto the palace grounds, she exchanged nods with Invel. The Drow was her backup plan but she'd be too distant for him to protect her from any kind of sneak attack.

The Malniet patriarch came into view, as did the underling who stood roughly at the same distance from the meeting point as Invel did. She and Styrris locked gazes and maintained their connection until they stopped a couple of feet away from each other. He was all in black with silver trim and looked like a freshly made zombie or vampire with his severe cheekbones and sunken eyes.

Cali nodded. "Patriarch Malniet."

"Leblanc." He replied,

He's trying to provoke you. Let it pass. "Have you considered my offer?"

"I have."

She desperately wanted to slap his face but restrained herself. "And?" *Do you want to be a conversational minimalist, scumbag? Two can play that game.*

Let me ice him, Fyre suggested mentally. *We can end this right here. He'll never see me coming.*

But we won't get what we need from him then, she replied. *So, no. Now shush.*

"One battle," Styrris answered. "Three on three. There's no reason for any of your other allies to die because of your foolishness."

Which means he doesn't have all that many people he can rely on, Fyre observed.

Cali agreed with and ignored the Draksa's comment. "Accepted. When?"

The patriarch sighed as if discussing the details was exhausting or irritating for him. She hoped it was both. "Saturday night."

"Well, give me a second. I have to check my social calendar." She looked up and pretended to think, and Fyre's laugh echoed in her mind. After a moment, she returned her gaze to her enemy and said, "I'll have to move some things around but it's doable."

"Until Saturday, then." He turned on his heel and strode back the way he'd come.

"You know," she called, "you could simply give me the information I need and we can skip the part where people bleed and die and your house is humiliated."

He didn't reply. She hadn't expected him to and simply shook her head and retraced her steps, collecting Invel as she passed. Fyre continued to fly high above and kept an eye out for any dangers that might await them. Emalia opened the door as they approached, and Fyre swooped through it behind them.

When it closed and they were all safe again, Cali sighed with relief. "Well, that sucked."

"I hate that guy," Fyre growled.

The older woman laughed. "Styrris Malniet has evoked that reaction in many people before you and will doubtless continue to do so for the rest of his life."

"Which might not be that long," Invel added.

Cali shook her head. "He won't fight himself. Surely he understands his limitations better than that."

The Dark Elf shrugged. "For you, this is a means to an end—getting what you need to free your brother. But from his perspective, it's a literal existential crisis. If House Malniet loses, it will be seen as weak. If it's seen as weak, others will challenge it. It might take a week or a month, but the family won't survive a loss for long. And whoever defeats them won't want the displaced patriarch hanging around."

She considered that information, which she hadn't understood before. It cast Styrris's actions in a fresh light, one she could better understand. It also held implications for what was to come. "So...if he thinks it's life or death, he'll do everything he can to ensure that we don't make it to the fight on Saturday."

Emalia nodded. "Yes, that seems logical."

Cali sighed. "Okay. We stay in the house except for essential things. No one travels alone. Use some of those gems Tanyith found and hire guards for the grounds. Fyre and I will go back to New Orleans and let Tanyith and Zeb know what's up. From here on out, we're in battle mode."

CHAPTER FIFTEEN

When Kendra had called and offered to buy him lunch, Tanyith had jumped at the chance to see her. While her responsibilities had slowed a little lately, Cali's absence meant he spent more time at the tavern than he'd expected to. If it was merely a job, he wouldn't have made it such a priority, but he owed Zeb more than only the minimum.

He portaled into an alley next to the small restaurant. It was almost literally a hole in the wall. The businesses on either side had gobbled part of what should have been this one's space, so the tiny eatery had only enough room for a row of two-seater tables along the right-hand side and a walkway up to the counter at the back. Kendra was already inside and waited at a table near the middle. She was dressed in detective casual, a neutral blue blouse under a brown leather jacket. Diners occupied every other chair except the one opposite her, and several people stood in line to order food for takeout.

He kissed her cheek and sat. She pushed two hot dogs loaded with toppings across to him. The first was a Chicago dog adorned with the hottest sport peppers he'd ever tasted. It was his favorite item on the menu. The other was a local "gumbo dog," which was andouille sausage with a dark gravy that carried all the flavors of the traditional New Orleans dish. That was his second favorite.

She'd selected the same and was halfway through her first already but paused to gesture with her chin. "Eat. We'll talk after."

Tanyith laughed and complied. If nothing else, his girlfriend was practical. He assumed her experiences as a police officer made her that way and he'd been told by friends with military experience that eating whenever possible was an absolute rule. She leaned back with a sigh when her food had vanished. "That was good stuff."

"Absolutely. The perfect choice for a lunch date."

"We live together now. We're not dating anymore."

"So, the glamor's gone that quickly, huh? How disappointing."

They laughed and Kendra's smile faded. "Will you need to fight again? In New Atlantis?" When he'd told her the story of the battle against the Atlantean gang, she'd seemed more worried than usual. *Maybe cohabitating is deepening both her feelings and her concern.*

He shrugged, ran a napkin over his lips, and used it to brush crumbs out his goatee. "I'm not sure but it's likely."

"Will it be more dangerous than the last one?"

"There's no way to tell, honestly. On the one hand, we'll fight the best of the best again. But on the other, they won't be able to choose a battleground filled with traps. So it's kind of a wash, at worst, with the possibility that it'll be better." He stretched across the table and touched her knuckles to stop the continuous drumming of her fingers. "What's up, Kendra?"

She sighed and pulled her hand out from under his. Leaning back, she folded her arms and shook her head. "It bugs me that I can't help you. I mean…helping is what I do, you know? And for you, who's more important than the average person to me, I can't do a damned thing." She managed a crooked smile as she delivered the understatement. At least he hoped it was an understatement of his importance to her.

"Which irritates you because you're my girlfriend or because you're a detective?"

"Some of each. More of the former. Probably."

"I wish I could say or do something to make that better but you know I can't. I gave my promise that I'd back Cali—"

"I'm not asking you to do anything in particular," she interrupted. "I only wanted you to know why I'm being… well, the way I'm being."

"I hadn't noticed any change." He had time to pull away before her open palm slapped on his arm but decided she needed the outlet. Still, the blow hurt. He laughed. "I always forget how strong you are."

Kendra shook her head but a smile began to form on her face. "Perhaps you need more regular lessons." She stiffened suddenly and looked over his shoulder, and he twisted to look at the doorway, wondering what had tweaked her instincts.

A person he recognized stood there—a man he had last

seen in the Zatora mansion. Aiden Walsh raised his hands to show they were empty and said, "There's no need to get angsty. I come in peace."

Tanyith shook his head. "Yeah, sure you do. What do you want?" He was ready to cast defensive magic and even jump up and attack the mage if necessary.

"Only to talk." He hadn't left the doorway and was half in and half out of the restaurant.

"Not here," Kendra replied sharply.

He nodded. "Go to the bar two doors down. They'll be open. I'll be there in a minute."

The other man gave a sharp nod and headed out the door. He rose and turned to say goodbye to Kendra, but she was already striding past him. "Are you coming, Tay? I'd like to hear whatever story this chucklehead has to tell. He's the one you were searching for, right?"

Damn detective instincts. She remembered his description. "Yeah, right."

"Good. Finally, some answers. Let's go beat him until he talks." At that moment, he couldn't be sure she was kidding so he followed more quickly than he otherwise might have.

The bar was a dive but was still about twice the size of the hot dog restaurant. Its door opened onto the narrow side of the rectangular bar, two silver stools with red vinyl padded seats only a foot away as they stepped in. The guy they sought sat at a rickety table in the back corner, a bottle of expensive bourbon and three shot glasses on the surface in front of him. His hands were also visible in what was doubtless another show of his harmlessness.

As if I'd be so stupid as to consider this man harmless after what he's done. Tanyith knew about his actions at the mansion and the way he'd killed the Zatora lieutenant and tried to frame Cali for it. He imagined Walsh had been involved in far more nefarious activities too but had only his instincts as proof. Still, it wasn't a gigantic leap.

He sat across from him, and Kendra took a seat at the next table at enough of an angle that a single gun couldn't cover them both. It would have been an excellent plan, except that the third person in their triangle was able to attack with a word and a gesture with both hands simultaneously. Still, it did ensure that one strike wouldn't suffice.

Walsh spoke first. "Okay, so I know you don't trust me. You have every reason not to. But I'll tell you that you should and explain why."

Tanyith shook his head. "Back up. Tell us why you were with the Zatoras. Oh, and since I doubt that Aiden Walsh is your real name, how about you share that with us, too?"

He nodded. "My name is Ozahl. I am from New Atlantis, that part was true. But when I got here, I didn't want to use my real name in case things went wrong with the gang."

"In case you burned too many bridges and ticked off too many people."

The other man chuckled. "That is…accurate. I wasn't as savvy then as I am now."

Kendra growled with open displeasure. "Oh, you're still ticking off folks left and right as far as I can see."

Aiden—Ozahl—glanced at her with a smile Tanyith remembered from the old days. "It's good to know I haven't lost my touch." He turned back and said, "So, I was with the Zatoras because it served my purpose to be with them. I was never interested in acquiring power here, even though I played the game on both sides. I went solo for a while in between. But all along, what I've really worked on is a way to accomplish things in New Atlantis."

He shrugged. "Well, nice catching up with you then. Good luck down there."

The man grimaced. "Okay…look, I get it. You have no reason to trust me. I'm very sure I said that already." He paused, looked annoyed, and blew a breath out. "The moment has come where our purposes intersect. You have interests in New Atlantis. So do I. We should work together."

Kendra snorted. "That's rich. What could you possibly offer?"

Ozahl didn't look at her and stared directly ahead. "Right now, Styrris Malniet is looking for ways to cheat. I have it on good authority he'll accept Leblanc's challenge for one decisive battle. So, he'll seek the best champions he can buy and work at eliminating her, her friends, and any potential allies he knows about or finds out about. And, last time I checked, House Leblanc didn't have an abundance of resources down there."

Tanyith scowled. *Unfortunately, he's not wrong.* "Let's say, for the sake of conversation, that you're at least partially correct. Where are those 'intersections of purpose' or whatever you called them, exactly?"

Ozahl leaned forward and put his forearms at the edge of the table. "Here's the thing. My goal requires the fall of a noble house. I don't particularly care which one. So, right now, I could be having this conversation with Styrris Malniet."

Kendra bristled and interjected, "That sounded like the kind of threat that might get you thrown in jail."

"I know." He nodded. "So that's one more assurance of my genuine desire to work with you. Anyway, I think Styrris is a scumbag and the head of a family of equally reprehensible scumbags. In fact, the only person in New Atlantis I admire less than him is the Empress. So, we have a common goal. The defeat of Malniet."

He considered the man's words for a moment, then replied, "And how do I know you're not playing double agent on his behalf already? It seems like it would be much safer to lock you up."

Ozahl sighed and raised his hands in a gesture of helplessness. "There's no way for me to prove that to you except by my actions. And to get there, you'll have to agree to work with me."

"What do you propose? Specifically, that is. The Aiden Walsh I used to know was capable of being specific."

The other man grinned at him and again, it was the familiar smile he remembered. "Well, I think we start by getting as many people as we can to watch out for trouble against Leblanc and to locate those who Styrris might select as champions. We counter those who could target her and we detain the potential hirelings until after the fight."

"That's kidnapping," Kendra observed mildly.

"Yeah." He shrugged. "But it's better than the alternative —and better than letting the top people fight your girl, right?"

Tanyith nodded. "You make sense. I agree. We do share interests here. But if you step out of line, history or not, I'll kill you myself."

"That's only fair." The man extended a hand and he shook it. "So, shall we get started? I know where two of the most likely candidates for Styrris's team live."

CHAPTER SIXTEEN

The Vimana's training room was amazing. No other word sufficed. Copper-colored metal made up all the surfaces, and lights set in the peaked ceiling cast odd shadows on the areas below. Cali had seen most of the other rooms on her last visit but this one was only for combat drill and had been omitted from that tour.

She had chosen to wear her black uniform with the sheath for Defender strapped across her back, her knives at her waist, and her bracelets on her forearms. She and her opponents formed a diamond with each at a point. On her left stood Cara Binot, who wore "agent casual"—faded blue jeans and a khaki military t-shirt with combat boots. Casually, she flipped and twirled her daggers, Angel and Demon. Diana's second in command had recently cut her hair almost to the scalp, and it gave her kind of an Ellen Ripley from *Alien 3* look.

Nylotte's lips were twisted in one of her familiar sardonic smiles, which always seemed to judge and find no end of lack. The Drow wore black leather, as usual, but had traded her jacket for a tight-fitting tunic. Her white hair was bound in a high ponytail barely visible over the top of her head. She had similar weapons in similar positions to Cali's.

At the fourth point of the shape stood Diana Sheen. Her outfit mostly matched Cara's, only she'd selected black jeans instead of blue. She also wielded a sentient sword, Fury. In the hours since Cali's arrival, the four of them had discussed the benefits and pitfalls of dealing with willed weapons.

Now, it was time for practice. Atop a pedestal in the corner of the room, up about six feet in the air, Rath the troll sat with his legs crossed and a smile on his face. He was about three feet tall and his most notable features were his wide grin and the purple hair sticking up in all directions from his scalp. She hadn't seen Max yet but looked forward to renewing her acquaintance with the troll's canine companion.

Nylotte was Diana's mentor and had also agreed to teach both Cara and Cali at different times. The Drow had naturally taken control of the group as soon as she'd arrived at the ARES Agents' base, and the current session was her idea. "We'll give Cali some practice dealing with attacks from multiple vectors." The Dark Elf locked eyes with her. "We'll go slow at first. All of us are skilled enough that if we cut you, it won't be anything we can't fix with a healing potion. Rath has a supply up there so you shouldn't worry about that. What you need to concentrate on is deepening your connection to your sword. Time's running out for you to build your bond before your big fight."

She scowled. "I wish you'd quit calling it a big fight. It

sounds like I'm about to break up a relationship rather than battle for the existence of a noble house."

Cara laughed. "She's right. It kind of does."

The Dark Elf shook her head. "Focus, people. Let's begin. Only weapons at first, no other magic."

Cali couldn't allow them all to attack her at once, so she'd need to stay in motion and use one to block the others as best she could. She darted to her left and drew the sword with her right hand and the dagger with her left, and Cara advanced to meet her. The agent swung at her face with one dagger and drove the other forward in an attempt to stab her in the chest.

She stepped away from the first and blocked the second with an inside-out circle of her smaller blade. Defender whipped up at a diagonal, aimed at her foe's hip, but Cara skipped out of the way before it got anywhere near her. Cali continued to move in the direction of the swing and twisted to face Diana, who had slipped in for her attempt. Fury snaked out in a quick thrust at her stomach, and she drove the hilt of her dagger onto it to direct it down as she dodged. The Drow's arrival frustrated her counterattack. She ran forward to disengage from the cluster and spun to meet the next assault.

It came from Nylotte, whose sword slashed across her at waist level. Cali blocked it with a downward stab of Defender and countered with a slice at the Dark Elf's face. As Diana rushed in from the right, her sword had already begun to move into place to block the other woman's before she'd fully processed the danger. She'd sent her magic questing toward the weapon at the beginning of the battle but without much direction, simply seeking a way in.

Apparently, it had discovered one. The movements around her seemed to slow and give her more time to react and respond. Her movement speed stayed the same, though, and she had the presence of mind to realize it was probably a function of the sword's magic.

The Dark Elf's call for the others to increase their pace negated the advantage after only a moment. *Damn her.* They crossed swords and daggers again and again, and Cali's predictive ability increased as they progressed. She could almost sense where the attacks would come from before they started. Just when she felt good about her skills again, Nylotte hurled a blast of lightning at her face from close range.

Defender jumped into the gap and absorbed the incoming magic with ease. Cali was very sure she'd been the one driving the motion but at this point, she felt as much like an extension of the weapon as she did the blade's wielder. In the back of her mind, barely below comprehension, it sounded as if someone was having a conversation. *Maybe those are the people who transferred themselves into the sword?* She didn't have time to consider it as the agents joined the magical assault.

She faltered only once—a clumsy move as she tried to shift position—and Fury scored a line of fire along her leg. A quick riposte drove Diana back but the wound would spell her defeat before too long. She took a step back to evade and the voices in her head united to shout a warning. Reflexively, she whipped Defender around her in a circle in time to deflect the throwing knife Rath had hurled at her from behind.

Nylotte shouted, "Hold," and everyone froze. Cali

panted, dripped blood onto the floor, and eyed her opponents warily. All three wore approving smiles, and in only a moment, the troll was at her side and handed her a healing potion. She took it with a nod of thanks and drank enough to make the cut vanish. The Drow asked, "So, what took place between you and the sword?"

Cali shrugged. "Things slowed for me. I could almost see what would happen before it happened. Then I noticed voices talking but…like, too low for me to hear exactly what they said. Until they all yelled at me to block."

Cara nodded. "That sounds familiar."

"Yep," Diana replied. "That's how it works for me too. Although Fury's not prone to talking to itself."

The other agent rolled her eyes. "There are times my two won't shut up. Usually at the most annoying moments."

The girl laughed. "So good, I'm not going crazy. Nice to know. I was worried for a minute there. By the way…" She twisted to look at the troll. "That was a dirty trick, dude. I thought we were friends."

Rath laughed, grinned, then did an excellent interpretation of Yoda from *Star Wars*. "One who helps you learn a true friend is."

"Plus, he'll take any opportunity he can get to show off his knife-throwing skills," Diana added. "Don't let him convince you to bet on a contest. He's unbeatable."

Nylotte sighed. "Can we get back to the rather important topic at hand, please?" No one looked particularly repentant but they all turned their attention to their teacher. "So, your sword has begun to work with you. That's good. But there's still a long way to go. We'll train every morning and afternoon while you're here. The rest of the time, you'll get some sleep and discuss strategy and tactics with Diana and Cara."

Cali nodded. She was incredibly lucky that they'd agreed to help her yet again, and she would do anything asked of her without question. *Although next time, I'll keep an eye on the troll.*

"Kayleigh is working on some stuff for you as well," Diana added. "We'll see what she comes up with before you go too." She had reached a level of acceptance with the agents that permitted her to know Diana was referring to the woman she'd previously only known as Glam.

"Awesome. I love gadgets and gizmos."

Cara grinned. "Me too. It's why I joined."

Diana frowned. "You said it was because you thought I'd be a fantastic leader."

The other woman shook her head. "I lied. It was for the toys."

Cali laughed right up until the moment that Nylotte said, "Rest break's over. Time for round two."

CHAPTER SEVENTEEN

Usha had donned her Champion's gear for her visit to the palace. The grand structure in the center of the domed city gleamed extra brightly as if the universe knew it might be her last time inside and wanted to make it a special experience. When the Empress's summons had come, it had been a relief. Even though she only had failure to report, she generally preferred to avoid delaying important events, whether good or bad. Still, her steps slowed involuntarily as she approached the entrance.

Four guards awaited her, with Gwyn at their head. The seneschal wore formal dress, a gown that reached to her feet in the palace's particular shade of blue. The way she stood—with her hands clasped behind her back and precisely on the threshold of the building so the visitor would have to stop on the outside—conveyed a definite sense of ritual. *It's symbolic and not a particularly good sign.*

She'd discussed the situation with Danna after they'd recovered from the battle, and the other woman had concurred that it was highly unlikely the Empress would kill her outright. The odds were good that she would leave the palace alive, although no solid bets could be placed on her fate thereafter. The possibility existed that things would go better than that, but she liked to make sure she considered the least appealing outcome to any given challenge.

Danna and her boyfriend—who she hadn't yet had the chance to meet—were somewhere in New Atlantis at the moment, ready to support her if she needed to run. The offer had been unexpected and her former second in command had insisted that she agree to it when she'd tried to demur. Her argument that she didn't want to taint her friend with her failure had accomplished exactly nothing. *That's genuine friendship, not like what Shenni has offered me lately.*

She halted in front of the seneschal and nodded respectfully. "Gwyn."

The older woman returned the nod. "Usha."

"Will I regret leaving my sword with you?" It was as close as she could get to asking if she'd be likely to survive the encounter.

A look of pain flickered across Gwyn's face. "Every piece of information I have tells me that you won't. But it's irrelevant. Your Empress has summoned you. You will hand over your weapons. All of them."

Without taking her gaze from the other woman's, Usha removed her daggers, her sword, and the other dangerous items from her uniform. Again, she was forced to trade her boots for another pair. After completing her disarming, the guards surrounded her, and Gwyn led her through the building on the most direct path to the throne room. Along the way, she made plans for how she would escape if it suddenly became necessary. It was merely an exercise to occupy her mind, though. If the Empress decided to eliminate her, death would find her before she had any idea it was coming.

They stopped before the high doors that separated the throne room from the hallway. While she waited, she studied the carved wood of the panels in front of her, which told the story of the early days of New Atlantis in a series of pictures that connected to some of the formative stories of her childhood.

She wondered what she'd see when the doors opened. Whatever lay behind them—unless it was an executioner with a giant ax—she still wouldn't know her future. The Empress would be within her rights to kill her in private or in public or to celebrate her in either of those ways. She snorted inwardly. *But somehow, I don't think she's likely to celebrate.*

Her best guess was that Gwyn was correct and she'd survive the encounter with her monarch. The older woman didn't seem tense enough to carry the secret that she was about to die. Of course, she might not know. Usha could have endured mental debate for hours in the throes of that argument, but the opening of the passage into the throne room forestalled any further consideration.

The room turned out to be neither full nor empty. A representative of each of the noble houses appeared to be present judging by the colors and insignia on either side of the carpet she was escorted along. They weren't the patriarchs and matriarchs, given the quality of their clothing. *So, public, but not so important as to require the most powerful audience. That adds weight to the survival part of the scale.*

The guards stepped aside as they reached the base of the dais to allow her to step to the edge of the staircase. She gazed at the Empress, who sat on her throne and stared at her in return. The dark tentacles that formed her hair moved slightly of their own volition. She'd always found them beautiful but now, the motion made her vaguely queasy. The frown on her monarch's face was enhanced by her stark makeup and the crown and torc she wore. *Damn. She went all out. That's a weight on the less desirable side of the scale.*

Conversations inspired by her arrival dwindled to silence. The Empress, always a master of dramatic timing, waited until it had become uncomfortable to break it. "Usha, Champion of New Atlantis, we welcome you. Please give your report." Her voice held no emotion, only flat disregard.

Usha's already straight spine stiffened. She bowed formally, the appropriate response to being recognized by the Empress. "I regret to share the news that Matriarch Leblanc managed to defeat the strongest fighters we had to offer. She has acquired powerful allies, and despite our best efforts, she survived. We have agreed, as is proper, to cease our endeavors in New Orleans."

"Disappointing." She shook her head and turned her gaze away as if to consider her champion's fate. *Dramatics. Equally disappointing, Shenni.* Another plus for the survival side, though. Posturing was unnecessary if she was about to be removed. As monarch, the other woman didn't need a reason. Finally, she looked at her again. "We trusted you to take care of a relatively simple task on the surface and somehow, you failed." She shook her head again and shouted, "Clear the room."

In moments, only Usha, Shenni, Gwyn, and two guards remained. The Empress fixed her with a hard look. "I was pleased to name you Champion years ago. Yours was a grand story—the rise from virtual nothingness to handily defeat every other contender. It seemed as if it shouldn't be too much to ask for you to secure the city for me. But you failed. I cannot countenance failure. It's bad for my image." She smiled slightly and in it, Usha caught a hint of the woman she knew and had once loved. It vanished as quickly. "There's only one way to make it right. One chance to stay in my good graces."

This was probably the moment where Usha was expected to say, *Anything, my noble, beautiful, brilliant, all-powerful Empress. Name it, and it will be yours.* But she couldn't force herself to do it. The perfect relationship they had once shared wasn't only damaged, it was broken. And while there might have been a way for her monarch to repair it, she hadn't chosen to. Instead, she'd doubled the distrust.

"And what is that, my Empress?" She did manage to keep her voice mostly neutral and spoke rather than snarled the words, even though it was difficult.

Shenni shrugged as if the Champion's feelings didn't matter to her in the least. "Kill the Leblanc girl before she fights the Malniets. Fix your mistake by serving the needs of a true noble house. Once you have accomplished that, I can send others to New Orleans and find another useful task that demands your skills."

Usha took offense in several distinct ways that competed for the title of greatest outrage. First, the other woman treated her like an amoral hired killer. She had never been that and would never be that. Second, she suggested the Malniets were somehow nobler than the Leblancs simply because they were allied with the Empress at the moment. *I wonder how long that'll last once she's taken what she wants from them. Days, not weeks, I would guess.* Finally, any tasks Shenni might give her after she'd debased herself wouldn't be ones appropriate for the Champion of New Atlantis. *Hell, I wouldn't have done that when I was poor and fighting only for survival.*

She cleared her throat and replied, "With all regret, Empress, I cannot do that." She added silently, *It's against everything I believe in and everything I thought you believed in.*

The monarch nodded. This result couldn't have been unexpected and her words sounded carefully rehearsed. "Very well. You remain Champion of New Atlantis with all the rights and responsibilities associated with that position. But henceforth, we will not recognize you. Begone, Usha."

As she spun on her heel and marched toward the doors, the guards rushed ahead to open them. She sensed Gwyn behind her, ready to interpose herself should she lose her mind and attack the Empress. *As if I would be so stupid. As if there aren't traps on the stairs, or archers in the walls, or some other way to kill me before I took three steps.*

Her escort didn't speak to her as they retraced their path to the entrance. Usha collected her weapons and traded her borrowed boots before she straightened to face the seneschal.

"I don't know what she's up to, but I don't think it'll work out well for her. If she changes—" She stopped with a small frown. *Changes what? Her mind? Her personality? Her beliefs? What would it take?* She shook her head and continued. "If she becomes the person she was—the person I can believe in—please find me."

The woman's face was hard as if she held emotion back. Usha wanted to think regret at her dismissal caused the expression, but it could as easily be outrage at her disobedience. She nodded. "I doubt such an event is likely to occur, Champion. Be well and for your own safety, keep your distance from the palace."

Usha laughed. "Don't worry, Gwyn. I have no intention to return. This has become a house of lies and deceit, and we already had too many of those." She turned and as she strode away, she noted with surprise that something that had been clenched inside her for so long that she'd forgotten it existed had begun to soften.

CHAPTER EIGHTEEN

Danna waited impatiently and drummed her fingers on the table at the dim restaurant in the outer circle of New Atlantis. Ozahl had made the successful argument that he should be the one to keep an eye on the palace in case Usha raced out of it with the Empress' guards on her heels. He'd be able to act with the element of surprise, while she would easily be connected to her former boss.

Former. It's so weird. Losing the battle wasn't an issue for her. She and Ozahl still possessed all their options for the final actions in their game. They might yet manage to eliminate both Leblanc and Malniet but would almost certainly be able to at least capture one or the other. Her boyfriend had already taken the right steps to co-opt Leblanc's people into their cause because it truly was their cause as well. That's what made it all so perfect.

Still, the waiting sucked. She'd requested only a single drink upon her arrival an hour before but had handed over extra cash to ensure the server wouldn't object to her occupying the back table and not ordering. The meal would be a celebration of one kind or another. A farewell to a wonderful partnership if Usha chose not to join them, or the start of something fantastic if she did. Either way, she didn't want to diminish her appetite ahead of time.

She brightened at the sight of the figure who stepped through the door. The delay had clearly involved stopping to change clothes as she couldn't imagine Usha had met the Empress in the casual blouse and black jeans she now wore. She waved and was rewarded with a thin smile. The other woman moved like a warrior as she traversed the distance between them, weaving gracefully through the mostly empty tables to her place in the back.

Danna gestured at the seat next to her. "So, the look on your face tells me things didn't go so well. On the other hand, you're not covered in blood so clearly, cutting your way out of the palace wasn't required."

Usha snorted. "I might have showered."

She shook her head. "This is where I politely avoid making a joke about how you'd smell better if you had."

"Fair point."

After a moment, she let the smile she'd been holding back escape. "I'm glad our noble monarch decided not to free up the title of Champion." Which would have involved the death of the current holder of that position. "Did you make a deal of some kind?"

The server arrived, and the woman ordered dark rum before she leaned forward and spoke softly when they were again alone. "Shenni wanted me to kill the girl— outside the rules. To benefit a certain house with which she is allied."

It was easy to understand the references. "And you told her no?"

Her companion nodded. "I did. We lost, fair and square, and we can't work against the girl now."

Danna leaned back and crossed her arms. "That's a fairly generous interpretation of the situation. We're not permitted to harass her in New Orleans, certainly. But what makes her off-limits here?"

Usha chuckled. "Always the devil's advocate, aren't you? Because right is right and bending the rules to the breaking point isn't necessarily ethical in every situation."

She laughed. "So what's your plan now?"

The other woman sighed and shrugged. "Fix my house up. Maybe open a bar here."

The door opened again and Ozahl stepped through. Danna smiled. "Nah. The boring life wouldn't suit you. What if I had a better idea?"

Her ex-boss raised an eyebrow. "I'd listen."

Introductions went more or less as Danna had expected. The first reaction—to meeting her boyfriend—was polite and welcoming. The second—to the information that he was their mole inside the Zatoras—was greeted with far more suspicion and required them to gloss over some of the details, especially those involving actions against the Atlantean gang.

By the time they moved to the third revelation, she felt a pause was in order. She guided the conversation around to stories of growing up in New Atlantis while they ordered food and devoured it, each of them seemingly famished. *Or maybe we're all eager to get to what comes next.* When a tray of desserts to share arrived, the moment of truth came with it.

She cleared her throat. "So, about that better idea."

Usha nodded. "Is this something you two cooked up together?"

Ozahl smiled. "It's been simmering for a long time. While she was loyal to you, I was disloyal to...well, everyone in preparation for the end game. We're now on the cusp of the final act."

"I wanted to tell you for the longest time, but I couldn't," his partner added. "We both know you needed to chart your own path. Only now, when we've all wound up at the same place in the same moment, is it possible for me to finally share."

The woman sighed. "I understand but doesn't mean I like it. It makes me feel kind of stupid if I'm honest. But let the past stay in the past. What's your play?"

She grinned. "We'll become nobles."

Her former leader—*it still sounds weird*—laughed, then frowned. "Wait. You're serious?"

Ozahl nodded. "As a lightning bolt to the eye."

"How?"

Danna took a bite of the chocolate cake that was set before her and vaguely noticed the many ways in which the subtle differences between Atlantean cuisine and surface food manifested. In this case, it was an edge of sea salt she wouldn't have expected. She followed it with several sips of coffee while she put her thoughts in order and lowered the cup. "There are two possibilities. First, Leblanc loses and we swoop in to take her house."

Usha laughed grimly. "It's not all that likely, I've come to believe."

"Yeah. Betting against her seems like a bad idea. So we're working another angle. Ozahl has met with Tanyith, the one who's fought alongside her the longest. They've agreed to work together against the Malniets."

"Who will doubtless cheat all the way to the battle."

Her boyfriend laughed. "Who are already cheating and would continue to do so probably from beyond the grave if they could learn how to."

"The goal is to weaken Styrris's position from the shadows," Danna continued, "and when the outcome of the fight is known, move on whichever house is weaker."

"Or both." Usha said it like she'd been involved in the planning from the beginning.

Ozahl clapped briskly. "Exactly. Or both. *Damn*, it's good to finally talk to you in person. Danna said so much amazing stuff about you that it was hard to believe it, but I see it's all true."

The other woman flashed a quick smile at him before she returned her gaze to Danna. "So, you're asking me to be a part of this endeavor? To work for you?"

She shook her head. "To work with us. If we only score one house, you'll be the third most powerful within it after the matriarch and her husband."

Her partner barked a laugh. "You mean after the patriarch and his wife."

"He's having trouble accepting reality." She rolled her

eyes. "Anyway, third. But if we get two houses, the other one is yours, free and clear."

Usha sounded doubtful. "Just like that?"

Her friend spread her hands wide. "Just like that. We don't want to be separated anymore. We've already spent enough time apart to last a lifetime. And any new family will need allies."

Her ex-boss leaned back and sampled her dessert, a custard Danna was unwilling to try because it involved seaweed, and remained quiet for more than a minute. In the interim, she sensed her boyfriend's desire to speak but stopped him with a glance. The Champion of New Atlantis needed to make this decision on her own with no more persuasion than she'd already been given if she was to fully buy in. Danna knew this because aside from Ozahl, Usha was the best friend she'd ever had. She waited and felt like her entire life hung in the balance.

Finally, the woman spoke. "How far outside the rules will we go?"

Danna expelled a relieved breath at the use of the word "we." "All the way."

"We'll remove as many Malniets as possible," Ozahl added, "and as many of the people who might fight for them as we can find. The family members can choose between exile or death as they pose a threat to us later. Those who can be bought, we'll lock up until after the battle. They won't like it but they'll come around after we pay them out of the Malniets' accounts once they're gone."

"That plan doesn't work if Leblanc is the one who loses," Usha replied.

She shook her head. "Actually, it kind of does. That's

the two-house scenario. Even if Malniet wins, they'll be so reduced by our actions that they'll be ripe for a takeover. We'll move on Leblanc first and take Malniet on again while they're weak."

The other woman nodded. "You've planned this carefully."

"We have," the man replied. "For a long time. And it will work."

A frown crept onto Usha's face as she stared at her. "So I guess the only question is whether I can trust you now that I know you've been lying to me all along." A chill ran through Danna in the instant before her former boss smiled. "I'm screwing with you. I'm in. Let's kick Malniet ass and show the noble houses how a life of privilege makes you vulnerable."

She didn't add the words, but Danna sensed them nonetheless. *And let's show Empress Shenni too.*

CHAPTER NINETEEN

It was the second night since Aiden Walsh—*no, damn it, Ozahl*—had come out of hiding and convinced him that they had a common enemy. The two of them had sealed their partnership by capturing and detaining a couple of potential Malniet champions. Tanyith had worked at the tavern the previous evening, and the new arrangement had time to work on his subconscious to change his perspective from grudging acceptance to outright enthusiasm.

So what if it serves whatever purpose he wants? It also helps protect Cali and gets me the payback I so richly deserve. It's win-win-win all around. He stepped through the portal onto the New Atlantis dock with a spring in his step he immediately subdued lest his freedom from the effects of the sinister spell be noticed. At least one of the runners at the docks would be a Malniet watchdog. When he'd sent the request for a meeting to those who doubtless still believed they were extorting him, he assumed they'd probably have eyes on him from the start. *Which is why I finished all my planning beforehand.*

He was dressed inconspicuously in jeans, a t-shirt, a leather coat, and work boots. The outward appearance concealed the daggers hidden along his spine, one for a top draw a little below the collar of his jacket and the other at the bottom, ready to be pulled from his lower back. If they took his coat, he still had his magic and his reinforced footwear. On the surface, both Kendra and Sienna were on guard, as were those acting as their security details, and would be until the situation with the Malniets was resolved.

And tonight will be a big step in accomplishing that highly rewarding task. He wandered the short route from the docks to the Privateer Pub, pretended to have the weight of the world on his shoulders, and kept his head down and his pace slow as if he was reluctant to arrive. When he finally reached the restaurant, he stepped inside and walked to the bar. The same man with the impressive mustache who'd been there the previous time stood behind the curved wooden surface. Tanyith beckoned him to lean over so he could speak privately.

"You seem like a good sort, so I'll give you a heads up. The folks in the back probably aren't pleased with me." The flat expression he received in return confirmed that they were there and that they were being their usual disagreeable selves. "You might want to relocate the people closest to that section. Actually, if you wanted to be real smart, you should get everyone out of here as quietly as possible." The other man's gaze flicked toward the door to the back room, and he shook his head to warn him. "It's too late to alert them unless you're telepathic. But you don't look like a true believer, merely someone who is stuck providing a service they'd rather not sully their hands with. So, take care of yourself and your customers. Clear out."

The bartender nodded and moved to the far end of the bar where the pass-through was located. Tanyith turned and strode to the back. The man might still try to intervene, but that wouldn't be very smart. He scanned the patrons. Among them were only four seated alone, three men and a woman. Ozahl could be any of them, based on his proficiency with disguise. While the two in the rear room could pose a challenge for him without backup, the addition of his new ally should mean much better odds. He might have had a qualm about killing them but frankly, the combination of their actions and their status as an ongoing threat to him and his friends earned them whatever they got.

He reached the door, took a deep breath, and yanked it open. Finding a third person present was unexpected but not a concern since he had additional support as well. The blonde woman sat in the seat closest to him. Her face was even more freckled than he recalled, and she wore a sleeveless top that revealed her hard muscles. It was a good disguise for the level of magical prowess she possessed, given her ability to plant a spell on him.

The man he recognized was beside her and his goatee and mustache looked even wilder than they had before. *Maybe he's trying to hide the divots in his face.* Their new friend leaned back in his seat with expensive-looking boots on the table. He had an air of confidence about him and was dressed in a trim button-down shirt and fashionable trousers. The three looked like worker bees joined by a manager bee. He turned his attention to the one he hadn't met yet. "Who are you?"

The stranger took his feet off the table and rose. He stood a couple of inches taller than him and seemed to expect that his height would be seen as intimidating based on his expression. Unimpressed, Tanyith shrugged and waited quietly until finally, the other man said, "That's not important. What is important is whether you've done as you were told. We're tired of waiting."

"You mean you and your friends here?" He gestured at the two he'd dealt with before.

"Don't be a smart guy. Did you burn the club?"

"Yeah. Just before I came here. I used gasoline all around the outside. It went up like a matchbook."

The seated man shook his head. "You don't smell like smoke or gasoline."

Tanyith responded with a thin smile. "I'm sorry. If I'd known that was your preferred choice of perfume, I would have put some on. I subcontracted the job. I'm not an idiot."

A grunt issued from the standing man. "That remains to be seen. And the council?"

"I already gave you all I have except for one thing. They're ticked off and they will step into the void the gang left behind to make sure no one messes with the city. New Atlantis is done there."

Another grunt followed. "That also remains to be seen. And the last part? It doesn't seem like you did as you were told from what I hear."

Tanyith shrugged. "Cali wouldn't have lost that fight, no

matter what I did. She was too well prepared. So I'll do it when it matters—if I have to."

The woman chuckled. "Oh, you have to. If you want your little women to be safe."

He made a shooing motion toward her but kept his gaze locked on the big man. "Quiet. The boss here is talking. Also, I didn't get your name, boss. Or should I simply keep calling you boss?"

With a sigh, the man opposite him shook his head. "You're way too clever for your own good. Maybe we need to teach you a lesson. Kill one of the girls you love."

"Yeah, a lesson." He sighed. "That makes sense." He raised his hands and discharged a line of lighting spread wide enough to encompass all three of them. The sudden appearance of a shield separating them from him wasn't a huge surprise. The powerful blast of force that hurled him through the surface behind him was.

Fortunately, the thin wall was decorative rather than structural. He struck a table, which promptly flipped and dumped him onto the floor. Because he'd been ready for some kind of reaction, he was able to make sure his hands touched first and protected his skull as he landed. He scrambled sideways to avoid any incoming blasts but none appeared.

Carefully, he rose and drew his daggers. The three used the doorway to enter the conspicuously empty main room. The big man nodded. "So. You planned this. Your women die tonight."

Tanyith shook his head. "I don't think that'll be as easy as you imagine. But you'll never know, of course, since you won't leave this place alive." He turned to the woman, who looked slightly confused. "Yeah, that spell is long gone so you can quit trying."

The other man who'd been irritating from the start opened his mouth to speak and he hurled a dagger at his face. The man yelped and conjured a shield barely in time to avoid swallowing the weapon involuntarily. Tanyith charged the woman and a burst of magic issued from the far corner of the room as Ozahl stepped out from behind a veil. The shadow blast struck the big man in the head and he fell instantly. *Surprise attacks are always handy.*

His adversary hurled a ball of flame, and he ducked hastily enough that it only singed him. The smell of burning hair was nauseating, and he managed a better effort to avoid the second one as he surged toward her. He stabbed forward with the blade in his right hand, but she responded with a shockingly fast crescent kick that knocked his attack off-target. Her other foot rocketed at his head and he had to dive to the side to dodge it. He pounded into the top of a table, rolled off, and found his feet quickly enough to evade the next baseball-sized orbs of fire she threw at him.

He tasted smoke and realized the structure had caught fire. Ozahl traded shots with the other Malniet, who remained upright beyond the woman. A serpentine path connected Tanyith with her position, and he raced along it and raised a shield to protect him from the next three fireballs she launched at him. He feinted as if to drive into her and she moved slightly to clear his approach to the other enemy. The man didn't realize he was there until his dagger dug into the back of his neck and unstrung his limbs, and he sagged into an untidy heap.

Tanyith twisted and raised a shield in the direction of the woman, but she stared at her chest in shock. A piece of wood from the wall protruded from it, presumably because Ozahl had used telekinesis to skewer her. She sank to her knees, still looking confused, and fell onto her side.

He glanced at the big man, the first one to fall. "Is he alive?"

His ally shook his head. "Nope. I had a lucky shot. His head was turned the right way—or the wrong way, depending on your perspective."

A hasty glance at the smoldering wood refocused him. "I guess we'd better get out of here before the place falls on us." He bent to retrieve his thrown dagger and headed to the exit.

Ozahl climbed over broken tables and met him at the door. "You know, I used to like this bar despite the name."

Tanyith laughed. "I can see that. Too bad it wound up infested by vermin."

They stepped outside and his companion sighed. "That's an excellent step toward our goal. Time to gather friends and take another one. Are you still in?"

He nodded. "Are you going after Malniets?"

"Of course."

"Then I'd say our shared interests continue," he replied with a grin.

The mage was quietly pleased as he led Cali's friend to a different part of the outer ring where he and Danna had taken an abandoned building as their own. Spaces didn't stay empty for long in the domed city, but there had been a death with no immediate family and things were a little up in the air at the moment. He assumed they had a week, tops, but they wouldn't need all of it.

Because after the battle between Leblanc and Malniet on Saturday night, we'll have a better house. A noble one. He'd skimmed cash from the Zatoras as a sideline to his other activities with and for them and had built up enough of a nest egg that they'd be able to hire any mercenaries they needed to establish their claim when the moment came. It would take the rest of the nine some time to come to terms with the move, but he wasn't worried. Once they were in, dislodging them would be virtually impossible. He'd ensure that it was.

Even though he trusted Tanyith, that trust extended

only to the intersection of the ring road with a spoke near their temporary abode but no farther. The two women emerged from the shadows at their approach and he put a hand on the other man's arm. "There's no need to worry. They're on my side, which means they're on your side now. I'm not asking for forgiveness, only understanding and professionalism."

Tanyith had stiffened at their appearance, and his nostrils flared as he processed the new information. Finally, he nodded and didn't quite growl his response. "Shared interests." The women were smart enough not to push and merely inclined their heads to acknowledge him.

"Are we good?" Danna asked.

Ozahl smiled. "Of course. We put a little pain on some of the stupidest beings ever to descend from the Malniet line. Honestly, I can't imagine what they were thinking giving those three any task at all." The comment made Tanyith chuckle, which was its intent. "So, what did you find?"

Usha cracked her knuckles. "A group of mercenaries operates out of a settlement they've claimed. A few of the younger Malniets like to hang out with them. It seems like they'd be a fairly good group for Styrris to recruit from."

Danna nodded. "If we target them, we take care of several things at once. We reduce potential champions, eliminate a Malniet or three, and maybe even keep one to sweat for information."

"I like it," Ozahl replied. "I can't see a reason not to. Does anyone disagree?" He didn't wait for a response. "No? Good. Let's go."

They'd taken a circuitous route to reach their destination to avoid attention along the way from any potential lookouts. A direct tube connected the section to the dock, but many of the settlements shared connections that didn't intersect the domed city and this was one of them. As a result, they passed through two separate living areas before they traversed a transparent cylinder that led to their target.

Ozahl was moved by being inside the tunnels again. It had been a long, long time since he'd used one, and it was entirely true to say he'd been a very different person then. The tubes had represented freedom, once. Now, they were simply a means to move from the place he wanted to be—the hub of New Atlantis—to somewhere he didn't care about. Even if they'd headed to the settlement his family had lived in, he would have felt the same. The old man was gone and someone new had returned in his stead.

The passage opened into what had once been an airplane fuselage. They had no way to know what to expect beyond the normal hodgepodge of reclaimed vehicles that made up the living areas that circled the central city. This section ran slightly downhill as if it were stuck on a rock or something. At the far end was a heavy wooden door, featureless except for a small spyglass set in it at head height.

"Quiet or loud?" Usha asked.

"Loud," Danna replied an instant before he did. The Champion of New Atlantis raised her hands and blasted the door inward with a bolt of force.

The mage was the quickest and had already lurched toward the doorway before the projectile had finished its flight. It crushed what was probably a guard, who stood outside another door opposite the first. This one was metal and also sported nothing but a small circle of glass. He shattered it and powered through.

It opened onto what seemed like the inside of a yacht set crosswise to their line of entry. A luxurious living room included several large couches and portholes that revealed the water beyond. He spared a moment of appreciation for whoever had made the vessel watertight before he raised a shield and moved to the right. His defense intercepted a blast of lightning that a woman in a black t-shirt, camouflage pants, and combat boots hurled at him. He sensed the others flowing into the chamber behind him and heard their shouts of alarm and anger as they were attacked in turn.

The initial fight was fast and brutal. He expanded his shield and raced at the woman to bulldoze into her. By that time, she had summoned her protection but it wasn't enough to prevent him from pushing her out the door behind her. He slammed it shut, cast a wall of force to keep it blocked, and spun. Tanyith had stabbed his opponent in the arm and launched a kick into the man's face. Usha and Danna fought as a team to consistently swap opponents at an unexpected moment to break through their defenses and overcome them.

He pointed at the door he'd secured. "We'll go this way." He dispelled his magical barrier and the entry fell open to show his enemy waiting for them. The woman's shield absorbed his lightning attack, but the force bolts from the other three catapulted her down the long corridor behind her. She landed hard, and Usha was there in moments to drive her head into the floor and ensure that she wouldn't join the fight anytime soon.

"Is there any way to know who's a Malniet and who isn't?" Ozahl asked,

Danna shrugged. "Not really. They like to play soldier so it could be any of them."

"All righty." He blasted the door at the far side of the hallway off its hinges with no immediate response. His normal option at moments like this would be to lead with a fireball but using such wantonly destructive magic underwater had limitations. Instead, he stuck his head cautiously around the corner and jerked it back as a blast of shadow careened into the wall. "It's an end room. They're in a corridor opposite this one."

He pointed at Danna and Usha. "You go forward. We'll keep going this way and meet you when we meet you."

"Be careful," his girlfriend replied, We're not invincible yet."

Ozahl laughed. "Against these idiots? Almost." As the others departed, he turned to Tanyith. "I'll go in shielded. They'll attack me and you come in and destroy them."

The other man nodded and the mage moved. He pushed a shield out from his skin in the shape of his body and tuned it with illusion so that he'd appear slightly away from where he physically was. It was an old trick but had made many of what might have been fatal attacks miss completely in the past. He surged forward and a beam of shadow followed him as soon as he entered the enemy's line of sight. The room was a small lounge with a couch and two chairs on the far side. He cursed inwardly at the fact that the larger piece of furniture rested against the wall. *It would have made good cover.* He stopped suddenly and dropped prone, and the beam passed over him.

He watched from foot level as Tanyith ran in and dispatched the enemy with a thrown dagger and a right hook. As he pushed to his feet, he brushed dirty carpet lint from his black pants and tried not to think about how quickly mold might form in a place like this. "Onward."

The hallway opened onto identical cabins, one after the next and all empty. They met up with Danna and Usha near the middle, which lacked a living quarter but had a ladder upward instead. It led to an opening in a higher deck. He shook his head. "Ugly."

Danna laughed. "You're getting conservative in your old age, love." She created a basketball-sized orb of lightning and threw it into the room, where it detonated and delivered bolts in every direction. Several thumps, both soft and loud, issued from the ceiling. Ozahl launched himself through the opening.

He landed in the middle of four twitching people. Five knives, one blackjack, and a nasty looking spiked club lay on the deck. Three of the fallen looked the same, the product of rough upbringings and the daily need to work for their survival. The fourth was different. His clothes were better, he had more flesh on his body, and his haircut had probably cost more than anyone in the settlement made in a week. As his teammates entered the room, he pointed out his find. "He looks like a pampered Malniet to me. What do you think?"

Usha pushed on the man's cheek with the toe of her

boot and elicited a groan. "It sounds right to me. Let's see what he has to say."

Fortunately, the wannabe mercenary was as spineless as they had expected. Once they had him tied to a chair, the first sight of a blade made him start to babble wildly. In short order, they had names and locations of other Malniet family members as well as his opinion on potential champions. Finally, and most importantly, he gave up the way to the bolt hole in the settlement where the remaining two Malniet cousins were hiding. When they offered him the choice of death or exile, he was quick to choose the latter.

Ozahl sighed. "They don't make nobles like they used to." He unbound the man, opened a portal, and pushed him through it. "I have friends on the other side. They'll keep him out of circulation until things have settled." He closed the rift and turned to the three mercenaries who sat bound on the floor and stared daggers at him. With a shake of his head, he observed, "It's not my fault you choose to consort with idiots. Don't blame me for your bad decisions."

"Will we kill them?" Usha asked,

He shrugged. "Let's see if they can make better choices." He knelt beside them. "Here's the deal. As of now, you're under contract. Your job is to stay here until Sunday. Don't leave the settlement. People are watching the docks, so we'll know if you break the rules. Obey, and you'll get cash at the end. It won't be a fortune but a good payday. Disobey, and you'll be in this hodgepodge pile of relics when we destroy it."

Their eyes widened and they nodded enthusiastically. Ozahl glanced at the others. "What do you think? Should we trust them?"

"Sure," Danna replied. "It's easy enough to locate and kill them if they disobey."

Usha added, "We can afford the risk."

He looked at Tanyith, who sighed. "Yeah. You're right. Let's limit the killing if these idiots will let us."

Ozahl clapped briskly. "Excellent. Now, it's time to find the other nobles and see what they have to share before they get to play 'Exile or Death.'"

CHAPTER TWENTY-ONE

Exhausted, Cali had collapsed after her first full day of training with the agents and Nylotte, and the day after had been worse. Today, there had only been a single session because her mind and body ached like they'd been through an old-school wringer—the kind she'd seen in *Bugs Bunny* cartoons on the Internet. She felt almost as boneless and her muscles were mostly jelly.

Tomorrow would be spent recovering, fueling herself for the battle to come that evening, and discussing last-minute details with her allies. Tonight would be all about the presents, plus a short celebration to send her off. She'd sleep in New Atlantis in what could be her final night as matriarch of House Leblanc.

Whenever her thoughts turned to that idea, she reined them in quickly. *What will be will be and worrying about it won't change it. Only planning can alter the outcome.* The words might have come from Nylotte, Sensei Ikehara, Diana, or even Zeb. All of them would have told her the same thing.

Which was why her walk through the base to Glam's lab was filled with hope rather than despair. Of course, the fact that Rath and his Borzoi buddy Max had waited outside her door to escort her and Fyre helped. The two cavorted and ran circles around her as they made their way through the wide corridors. The Draksa feinted and snapped as they passed. The whole exchange lifted her spirits considerably. Without question, she'd step onto the battlefield far better for her days spent with the agents.

They had even given her an honorary uniform—fatigue pants and a khaki shirt. Her boots were still her own, despite Diana's suggestion that she should allow Kayleigh to work on them. Hidden stilettos weren't her style, and her friends were right that she was more of a danger to herself than anyone else with a pistol, concealed or otherwise.

When they arrived, Kayleigh and Diana were waiting, seated on high stools next to a plastic-topped lab table. The tech looked younger than most of the other agents, doubtless in part because of her asymmetrical blonde haircut and deliberately noticeable makeup. The lead agent gestured for her to sit and said, "We'll try not to keep you for too long. I'm sure you're eager to get home and into your own bed."

She nodded. "I wouldn't have expected to feel that way, but yeah, I am." She climbed onto the stool at the end and Fyre found a corner to curl up in and supervise the proceedings.

Kayleigh stood in front of a bank of small lockers like those found in an amusement park or a health club. She stretched to one and pulled out a thin black vest. When she set it on the table, Cali noticed that it had a V-shaped line on it that protruded slightly from the fabric.

"Okay," the tech said, "since you're not likely to be shot at, this vest is all about resisting cutting. It won't stop a determined stab with considerable weight behind it, but it should turn anything that's less direct than that. Of course, each use will degrade its ability for the next, so consider it more a backup plan than your primary option."

Cali nodded. "What's that?" She pointed at the pattern she'd noticed.

The other woman grinned. "That is another secret weapon. Diana, would you care to do the honors?"

The lead agent rolled her eyes. "So, we thought you might not have found a use yet for the anti-magic deflector crystals we gave you. There are sockets in there for five of them. They cover them so they don't hurt you if they explode, which they've done on one or two occasions."

Kayleigh nodded. "They usually only crack. After we discovered they can do more than that, we started using guards. This isn't as fashionable as the ones I've made for the others, but I didn't have enough lead time to make it both effective and pretty, so I went with the first one."

She grinned. "Thanks for that."

The tech laughed. "I'm a gem. Everyone says so." She gestured at the object on the table. "Gem. Get it? Honestly, you people wouldn't know funny if it ran you over at high speed on a dark country road." She pushed the vest out of the way and placed four small spheres on the plastic surface. Each featured a stripe of a different color. "Red is incendiary. Blue, flashbang. Green, tear gas. Yellow, smoke. You set them off by shattering them on the ground."

The blonde turned to retrieve something else from the lockers behind her, and Diana pointed at the orbs, each of which would fit easily in her palm with room to spare. "Don't be misled by how small they are. They pack a serious punch. And you'll want to be way out of range if you use the tear gas. It sucks. I'm sure that Glam put us through extra testing rounds simply to be a jerk."

"Lies," the tech responded. "Science requires precision." She set a wide belt onto the table. "This will be an improvement on what you have. It has room for potions, sheaths, a pouch, and four places to slot your mini grenades in. You should practice and memorize where they all are ahead of time, though, until it's natural to retrieve the one you want." She pointed at the large round buckle, which displayed her family's symbol, a compass in blue and gold. "And an extra surprise if you need it." She pulled and twisted, and the buckle came off in her hand. "Press the center and…" She did so, and a curved blade popped out to cover the northern hemisphere of the circle. When she pushed again, the sharp part withdrew into the device.

Diana whistled. "Damn, Glam, we need some of those."

She laughed. "You're dangerous enough already."

Cali shook her head. "I can't imagine where I'd be likely to use such a thing but it feels good to know it's there."

Kayleigh took two small sheaths from the lockers, each of which had a curved handle protruding from it. She pulled one of them out to reveal a keen-edged throwing knife that looked to have been cut from a single piece of flat metal. "These go at your lower back where the agents often carry a backup pistol. I'm not sure if you're any good with them, but Rath insisted."

Diana laughed. "He would."

"I'm probably better with the knives than a gun, anyway," she said with a nod. "Which might not be saying all that much. There's no way I can thank you enough for all of this." Fyre sent a wave of affirmation, presumably at her assessment of her pistol proficiency.

The tech shook her head. "This is what I do for fun. No thanks required. And since the boss had little or nothing to do with it, there's no need to thank her, either."

The agent laughed and shrugged. "She's not wrong. This is all her."

Kayleigh grinned. "Okay, one more present—something I've been working on for the agents. I have to warn you, though, it's a prototype."

Diana groaned. "That means she's using you as a guinea pig. I'd run for the hills and fast if I were you."

"Nonsense," Glam quipped. "All my experiments are worthwhile for everyone involved."

Cali grinned at the banter as the boss replied, "Like the netgun?"

The woman waved a dismissive hand. "That wasn't so much an experiment as a field test of a terrible idea—your terrible idea, as I recall." She turned to face Cali and spoke over Diana's attempted reply. "So, we use capacitors on the agents' vests to deal with electrical attacks, both technological and magical. I didn't know how that would work with your magic and didn't have time to investigate, so those seemed like a bad option. Instead, I created this." She dug in the locker again and slid a disc about the size of a hockey puck to her. "It activates on impact and creates a magnetic field that attracts electricity."

"Have you tested this before?" Diana asked.

The tech shrugged. "Some smaller versions. It seems to work as intended."

The agent shook her head. "It's up to you, Cali, but if you do accept it, you should be ready to use it only in a dire circumstance. Even then, take my advice and throw it as far away from you as you can."

Glam sighed dramatically. "Luddite."

Cali took the object, along with all the other items on the table that Kayleigh helpfully slid closer to her. She slotted the spheres into their receptacles and positioned the sheaths. Finally, she put the disc in the pouch. At the tech's nod of approval, she shrugged and said, "You never know what might make the difference."

Diana stood and stretched. "True that. Now, how about one last meal and a drink before you go to show New Atlantis who's boss?"

She and Fyre arrived late at the Leblanc mansion. The house was quiet, and since Jenkins recognized her immediately, no alarms sounded. Somewhere along the line, this had started to feel more like home than New Orleans. Cali wasn't sure she liked it that way. Even if she won, she couldn't see spending her life in such a small place. She could still visit wherever and whenever she wanted by portals, but it wasn't the same, at least not in her head.

The Draksa leaned against her leg and she patted him absently. "I don't know, buddy. It feels weird to be here."

He snorted softly. "Things are changing. After tomorrow, nothing will be the same. Either we'll lose and be on the run, or you'll be getting ready to meet your brother." She appreciated that he didn't mention the other possibility of failure that resulted in one or both of them dying.

"I guess you're right. Well, I suppose a good night's sleep is the best thing we can do at this moment."

"Unless you might want some hot chocolate." He chuckled.

"You mean unless I want to give you marshmallows," she countered.

"I've heard they're good pre-battle food."

She laughed. "From who?"

The Draksa affected a haughty tone. "Reputable sources."

"Which reputable sources."

"Jenkins."

Cali shook her head. "Is this true, Jenkins?"

The disembodied majordomo's prim voice replied, "I cannot tell a lie. It is true, in fact."

They all laughed together and she raised her hands. "Okay, then. I bow to the collective wisdom of the room. Let's have some hot chocolate and marshmallows. We'll follow that classic advice—'Have sugar tonight, for tomorrow we may die.'"

CHAPTER TWENTY-TWO

Cali woke late and padded to the kitchen at lunchtime. Everyone else was already awake and seated at the big table. "Finally," Emalia said, "and just in time. Open a portal to the tavern."

Many appropriate replies flicked through her mind—most of them involving faux outrage at the continued lack of respect for her noble status—but she complied. Zeb looked impatient as he stepped through carrying a stack of pizza boxes with the name of her favorite slice restaurant in New Orleans. He deposited them in front of the others and took a seat. She let the portal close and joined him. Fyre nuzzled her foot from his hidden position underneath the table, and she patted him with her toes.

She tried to talk, yawned instead, and tried again. "Carb loading. I like it." Laughter and discussion ensued, and they spent an hour and a half having their version of the celebration from the night before. Thereafter, they relocated to one of the dens for more important conversation and outlined tactical situations they might face that evening.

She and Fyre shared a couch and the others pulled up comfortable stuffed chairs to make a circle.

Tanyith related his activities alongside Ozahl, Usha, and Danna, which had resulted in a reduction of both the available Malniets and the potential hires for Styrris. He promised more detail on how that had all come about at another time.

"So, the others plan to swoop in and take over Malniet when they're defeated, is that it?" Zeb summarized.

The man nodded. "Or Leblanc. They didn't hide that. But they also think we're more worth saving, apparently."

Emalia shook her head. "Or they'll move on both. We'll have to stay on guard after this is over for however long it takes things to normalize."

The ex-convict smiled. "Definitely. As a backup, I might have noticed where they've sent all the Malniets who choose to live. So, if they do decide we look tasty, we can retrieve them to cause trouble. Assuming they did exile them and not kill them once they got there, of course."

"Where is there?" Cali asked.

He chuckled. "Out of all the potential places where they could have stashed them, they chose an old Zatora warehouse I did recon on once. I noticed the view out the window, which shows the tip of the casino building in the distance. I think Ozahl must have used it for his purposes when he was with the organization. Nothing of note registered when I investigated it before."

Zeb folded his arms and looked satisfied. "That's a good backup plan. If you tell me where it is, I can get the magical council to put some eyes on it."

"Will do," Tanyith confirmed.

Emalia asked, "So, once you win tonight, what then?"

Cali stretched, patted Fyre's scales, and drew a sigh from the power-napping Draksa. "My main focus has to be saving Atreo. When we win, we come back here, activate all the wards to ensure we won't be disturbed, and take care of that."

Her great-aunt shook her head. "No. You'll need to rest first and eat, and wait for all the stuff that comes with the battle you're about to fight to fade. Your brother has waited for years. He can endure a little longer so you can do it right."

She frowned but had to acknowledge the truth of the other woman's words. "I hear you. We'll do it your way. Do we have guards?"

Emalia grinned. "We have purchased mercenaries and both Terriau and Jehenel are sending some of their best on loan for as long as we need them. Barring all-out war among the houses, we should be as well protected as we can be."

Invel, who had been mostly silent throughout the afternoon, added, "I'll assess the state of the wards and add power to those that can take it."

"I'll help with that," Zeb told him. "And I'll stay here until tomorrow at least. I'll only need a portal before you all go so I can get Valerie and close the Dragons." His tone was mild but she was sure he regretted not being part of the battle to come. He'd offered but she'd felt she owed it to Tanyith, who had been at her side all along, to be the one to accompany her. She'd given him an out but he had met her expectations by refusing to take it.

Cali stood and rolled her neck with a loud crack. "Okay.

Let's do the portal and then I'll get dressed. We leave for the big event in an hour."

Emalia slipped into her dressing room before she had a chance to start changing. Her great-aunt pointed Cali to a chair, pushed the clothes off a small table, and dragged another seat across from her. She sat, pulled her tarot deck out, and unwrapped the heavy cloth that protected them. "Let's see if the cards have anything to tell us."

She shrugged. "They knew about the Empress so could be useful."

The older woman nodded and shuffled. "We'll choose three. I'll move through the deck one by one and you tell me when to pull a card. The first is your past, the second your present, the third your future. Think about the battle to come."

Cali closed her eyes and let her magic slip free of its bounds to assist with her selection. The sound of the other woman working through the deck became her only sensation. When she felt a twitch from her power, she said, "That one." They repeated the process twice more before she opened her eyes.

Emalia wrapped the unused cards and set the bundle aside. On the table between them, face down, were three cards. "Ready?" she asked.

"Let's do it."

The first card to be revealed was a naked woman with a wand in either hand. It was upside down. Emalia's voice, deeper than usual, intoned, "The World, inverted. Lack of closure or something left incomplete."

She nodded and whispered, "Atreo."

Without reply, her aunt flipped the next card. It showed the same woman, her hands locked on the jaws of a lion. *Strength.* "Your present is about strength, both inner and outer. But remember that the card also refers to compassion, which is in itself a mighty force."

Cali didn't reply. She'd done all she could to build her strength in all the ways she knew how. It would either be sufficient, or it wouldn't, and nothing would change it now. But she would keep compassion in mind as much as she could under the circumstances.

The older woman placed her palm over the last card. "This, then, is your future." She turned it to display the High Priestess and chuckled. "Intuition and inner voice—it suits you well. Also often seen as a challenger to the Empress." She opened her eyes. "Trust your feelings, Luke."

The girl groaned. "Really? *Star Wars* quotes now before the biggest fight of my life?"

She grinned. "It was the biggest fight of his, too."

"I love you. Now, go away, crazy woman."

Emalia picked her cards up, her smile still in place. "Seriously, though. Trust yourself. You've got this."

Cali nodded and made a shooing motion with her hands, and as the door closed behind her great-aunt, she whispered, "Yeah. I got this. Sure." With a deep breath and matching exhale to push her worries away for a while, she rose and crossed to where her gear awaited her on the dresser.

First on were her uniform pants, solid and black. A tear

from a previous fight had been hand-stitched by Invel, who had proven to possess a wealth of unexpected talents. They had pockets in the usual places, plus thigh pouches with Velcro flaps.

Next came her socks and boots. The footwear was heavy, reinforced for kicking or blocking. They climbed to mid-calf and buckled instead of lacing. She'd often thought they were as fashionable as they were effective. When she'd made the mistake of sharing that opinion with others, a torrent of abuse about her inability to judge good fashion had resulted. It hadn't changed her mind, though.

She'd decided to wear the khaki t-shirt Cara and Diana had provided. Something about it gave her confidence, and she could use every ounce of that particular resource she could get. Next was the good luck charm Sensei Ikehara had given her. The thought of her teacher made her smile. He'd been overly generous to her from day one, and she was glad to wear his token into battle. She hoped to return it with its string of successful uses unbroken. Carefully, she pulled her hair out of the way of the chain and tucked the pendant under her shirt.

Her heavy uniform top came next. She buttoned it slowly from the bottom and secured the collar at her throat. A pin with the compass logo of her house went over the top button, and the symbol appeared on both arms and over her heart as well. The wide belt with the toys Kayleigh had provided wrapped at her hips, and she attached her daggers at each side.

Cali took each of the metal flasks that contained her potions and checked to ensure they were properly sealed. Healing and energy went into each thigh pocket, and she nestled an extra healing potion behind the prototype disc Kayleigh had given her and the glass orb Invel had provided in her belt pouch.

Her consciousness narrowed as she donned each item, bringing the battle ahead into clearer focus. She drew the vest over her head and strapped the sides tightly against her ribs. Satisfied with her progress thus far, she opened the top drawer of the dresser and retrieved the magic deflector crystals the agents had given her. The slots were perfectly sized for them and she snapped them into place one after the other. She put the safety fabric over them again when they were all secured.

Next, she looped the strap that held Defender's sheath over her head and a shoulder. She yanked it tight and checked the draw of all her weapons—sword, daggers, and throwing knives. Touching each of the grenades in turn, she reminded herself of their locations—incendiary, flash-bang, gas, and smoke. Finally, she set the charm necklace on top of everything with her last shield and light charms hanging from it.

She turned for the first time to the full-length mirror that stood in the corner. A woman with crazy hair looked out. With a sigh, she found the elastics she'd forgotten to use and pulled her curls back to tame them into a tight ponytail. When she looked in the mirror again, a warrior stared at her—one who would defeat one of the other Atlantean noble houses. And, she told herself, one who would free her brother. The warrior wouldn't stop until she accomplished these things, no matter what. She nodded at her reflection. *Game time.*

CHAPTER TWENTY-THREE

The slow walk through the city reminded her of the journey to the first battle with the Malniets only this time, her skin crawled like she had a target on her back that any number of people might be aiming for. Her only real defense was that any attack by the rival family at this point would be very visible and thus difficult to deny. *Which won't matter much to me if I'm dead.*

Fortunately, Fyre walked at her side. The Draksa continued a running commentary in her mind and pointed out potential assault vectors she might have missed while he generally maintained a watchful eye on their surroundings. It was useful both practically and emotionally. Keeping her head straight was more challenging than she'd expected. *Probably because I'm fighting for Atreo's survival too, not only mine.* The sense that her parents watched from somewhere added another stone to the rickety support of her emotional state.

She walked on the right, Fyre in the middle, and Tanyith on the left. He had dressed almost identically to her, save for the vest and the new belt. Emalia had provided him with a compass pin for his neck and even fashioned one as a necklace for the Draksa. The streets were more crowded than usual, and people stared at them as they passed. Some radiated support, some hatred, and many of the rest a simple bloodlust. A trailing line formed behind them as this fight would be a public show by decree of the Empress, who had also selected the venue—the Championship Arena.

The perfectly round structure was made up of a combat field at ground level with rising tiers of seating encircling it. Entrance passages existed at the four cardinal points. Cali and her allies would enter from the West. Styrris was required to be part of the Malniet procession, even though he wouldn't join the fight, and would enter from the East. The Empress herself was unlikely to attend, but a representative would probably be present to witness the conflict.

The arena came into view as they walked the ring road around the palace. It still lay at a distance, positioned along the next outermost circle that separated the noble houses from the rest. The same white stone that made up the Empress's seat of power had been used in the arena's construction. It appeared to glow in the diminishing light, and the illumination that filled the combat field spilled upward from the inside. She spoke only loud enough for Tanyith and Fyre to hear, although lip-readers or magical eavesdroppers could doubtless be found among the thickening crowd on the sidewalks.

"So, there it is. I'm starting to think this one battle to end it was a bad idea."

Tanyith laughed softly. "All your ideas are bad and yet they seem to work out. This will no doubt be the same."

Fyre snorted a frosty mist from his nostrils but made no effort to disagree. "You suck," Cali replied. "You both suck. How did I wind up with such jerks for friends?"

Into her mind, the Draksa observed, *Dumb luck, I guess. With the emphasis on dumb.*

"In other news," the man said, "how do you think the Malniets will cheat?" It had been a topic of discussion throughout the afternoon. Not if they would try to bend the rules to the point of breaking. That was a given. How they would do it was the ongoing question, especially under the allegedly neutral eyes of the Empress's representative.

She shook her head. "In every way they can. I can't imagine what it will be, though. I suppose we'll simply have to roll with it."

"Are you worried?"

Cali chuckled. That word was so inadequate to describe her feelings. "Hell yes, I'm worried. Anyone with a brain would be. Which, I guess, leaves you two out. You're lucky like that. It must be nice to be so unburdened."

They shared a laugh and lapsed into silence as the crowd grew bigger and they moved closer to the arena. She had a pair of primary concerns other than the cheating. The first was who or what Fyre would face. After experiencing Kraken, Giant Squids, and a Draksa of unusual size, she imagined something Lovecraftian showing up. The second and only slightly less worrisome issue was what spanners the Empress would throw into the works. When she'd decided to intervene, Cali hadn't been able to refuse.

Being the monarch has its privileges. But she didn't trust the woman for an instant. Shenni probably had a hundred ways to subtly skew the contest in the Malniets' favor.

Palace guards lined the last part of the walk. Her skin crawled as she passed between them and entered the darkened passage under the seating that led to the field. Fyre, doubtless sensing her agitation, sent a feeling of calmness and confidence across the channel that connected them. She took the hint and walled her concerns off, pushed them into the alcoves in her brain made for that purpose, and bound them there with crime scene tape. No matter how much magic she learned, her old habits sometimes remained entirely useful. By the time the tunnel finished, she was as ready as she could be.

Nothing could have prepared her for the throngs that filled the stands or the sight of three large circles painted on the grass—one in Leblanc scarlet, one in Malniet green, and one in the palace's unique shade of blue. Across the arena, her enemies entered at the same time she did, and far more of them were present in the retinue. Three figures in armor, another six in suits and gowns, and at the head of them, Styrris Malniet looked as fashionable and corpselike as ever.

She'd been instructed in the process by a missive from the palace that had been delivered that afternoon. They were to walk to the exact center, turn, and approach the royal box. The Empress's designee would address them and thereafter, the combatants would each enter a circle. The fights would be individual until the first death or incapacitation, at which time it would become a free for all.

Styrris had a smug smile on his face that grew bigger as

they approached. *Oh yeah, he's up to something.* The crowd sent support and vitriol at both of them, which made it feel like the start of a New Orleans Saints game. They turned in tandem and walked to where the representative of the palace was concealed behind a thick curtain. When they reached the appointed distance, the audience fell silent.

The fabric swirled aside to reveal three people standing between four guards. The sight elicited a loud gasp from the crowd, who then started to cheer. Cali only recognized the least important one from Emalia's description, but her forlorn expression confirmed she was Brielle Cormier, Styrris's new bride. Even though she hadn't expected the palace to be truly neutral, to have the wife of her foe in the royal box was a significant slap in the face. The woman's white gown, reminiscent of a wedding dress, was merely icing on that particular cake.

The next most relevant was the Empress's seneschal, Gwyn, who maintained an indifferent aspect with apparent ease. The older woman wore a tunic over a skirt, both of which were appropriate for the throne room and seemed overdone in this setting. A sword hilt protruded from the scabbard at her left hip.

The third person beamed at the success of her surprise. Empress Shenni stood in the center of the group wearing a broad smile as she waved at her people. Cali studied her as they all waited for the cheering to die down. The monarch was clad in a long blue robe but a glint of metal near her neck suggested she'd made the practical choice and worn armor beneath it. Her hands itched with the desire to attack her for her obvious bias and the public show of it, but the woman would doubtless be ready for that.

You'll have more than enough time to be a thorn in her paw later, Fyre whispered in her mind. *She doesn't matter right now.* She gritted her teeth and nodded.

Finally, the noise faded to a level that would permit the monarch to be heard. Her voice was incredibly well trained or magically amplified. "We are here today," she intoned, "in this place that has seen the rise of champions and the fall of houses, to witness the resolution of the challenge from House Leblanc to House Malniet. The participants have agreed to allow this battle to decide the dispute at hand. I am required to ask the challenged if they will set this combat aside and provide what has been requested."

She paused and Styrris shouted, "Malniet is not willing, Empress."

Shenni nodded. "And now, will the challenger agree to set this combat and their challenge aside?"

Cali shook her head. She hadn't been warned of this part—*imagine that*—but it didn't matter. "Leblanc will not, Empress."

A ripple of satisfaction passed through the crowd, who had come to see a fight, not a display of logical behavior.

"Very well," the monarch replied. "The rules are simple. Three opponents on each side. The battles begin in the circles but once one falls, separation is no longer required. Whoever is still standing at the finish wins. Combatants, take your positions."

She bowed toward the Empress she increasingly detested—only because it seemed like the smart thing to do —and turned on her heel. With quick movements, she pointed Tanyith to the circle most distant from the Malniet side of the arena, Fyre to the one in the center, and headed to the one farthest from where they'd entered. Hers and Tanyith's were a greater distance away from the royal box than the Draksa's in both directions, as the middle circle was set asymmetrically apart from the others.

As the six Malniet supporters and their patriarch faded to the back, their opponents entered the circles. Two wore armor consisting of leather and plates. A woman strode confidently toward Tanyith while a man focused on Cali. The two looked strikingly similar, right down to the way they moved, and carried sheaths that might contain swords and daggers. A figure in scale armor and a full helm carried a trident and stepped forward to oppose the Draksa.

That one probably has some experience with your kind based on the look, Cali sent to Fyre.

He's a trainer, he replied. *Some Draksa don't take to instruction very well, so they wind up in the hands of people like him.*

That doesn't sound good.

Let's simply say I'll be more than happy to kill him for you. His mental voice radiated fierce anger.

"Don't let your emotions get the better of you," Cali cautioned.

A note of mirth broke through the aggression coming from the Draksa. "Who am I—you?"

She shook her head and stepped into the ring opposite her opponent. His strong face showed respect rather than condescension. He was probably a hireling, not a family member. They exchanged nods, and she drew Defender with her right hand and a magical dagger with her left. Her foe drew a sword as well, and it shocked her to see it was a twin to her own but with a scarlet gem in the pommel.

Emalia's voice floated in her memory. "Ruby is the stone of House Rivette."

Empress Shenni had given her adversary a sword that could break hers. With grim certainty, she corrected herself. *No, not one that could break mine. One that has broken mine in the past.* Icy rage swept through her. *Damn that woman. Whatever she's up to, I'll make sure it doesn't happen.*

A translucent barrier snapped into place around the circumference of the circle, and she took a deep breath. The Empress's voice, now definitely amplified as it echoed throughout the arena, shouted, "Begin!"

CHAPTER TWENTY-FOUR

Her opponent moved with an economy of effort and sharp, small steps brought him closer to her at a measured pace. His body language suggested this was a comfortable environment for him, which made sense. It was highly likely many of the people for hire in New Atlantis had thrown their hat into the ring of the champion's contest that Usha had won. It was probable that the early rounds had been exactly like this—multiple bouts taking place at the same time before they'd been whittled down to the final few.

Cali released her magic to connect to Defender and the sword responded instantly to give her the sense of power at the ready. The voices returned, too inaudible to comprehend but engaged in some kind of discussion. She wondered if the inhabitants of the weapon talked among themselves constantly and whether that was what she heard, or if they slumbered and only awoke when called upon.

The idle thought flitted away as her enemy's sword

descended in a faster than expected diagonal chop. She skipped to the side to avoid it and launched a blast of lightning from her dagger that he caught on his shield, a translucent barrier of force that glowed briefly with the impact of her magic. She had tricks to play but would keep them in reserve since her opponent probably did too. No doubt the enemy was aware of her shield charm, at least.

She pushed energy into her muscles to increase her speed and strength. One of the voices from her blade increased in volume enough for her to hear it. *Force against force might break the sword.* She nodded at the warning. While she couldn't know if Defender was weaker because of its first shattering, she had already planned to do her best to avoid direct application of maximum power against it.

Her opponent matched her increased speed, and they traded attacks and blocks punctuated by discharges of magic. Nothing connected, but she had the sense that he was completely comfortable in this particular battle scenario in a way she wasn't. *Which means he's that much better than me—or he knows something I don't. Or maybe both.*

He deflected one of her swings with a spinning strike that knocked her blade aside. When he came out of it, his shield had been replaced by three knives that he flung at her face. With an undignified yelp, she threw herself onto her back to dodge them. She hurled her dagger blindly and cast a barrier of force over herself in time to catch the sword that stabbed down at her and managed to stop it a bare inch from her chest. Her foe put pressure on the weapon, so she pushed more magic into the shield. She swiped at him with Defender and he used his sword as a lever to jump up and over her.

The longer the stalemate continued, the worse for her. It was time for a trick. She whispered *"Iubar,"* and her light charm exploded into brilliance.

Fyre anticipated his opponent would expect him to take to the air immediately so instead, he charged as soon as the Empress's voice stopped. His serpentine approach caused the first blasts from his foe's trident to miss—or the trainer was faking it. *Either way, it doesn't matter.* He came within breathing range and launched upward as he sprayed frost at his foe. A shield snapped into place to absorb the blast, and he banked abruptly to avoid a branched burst of lightning that emerged from the tip of the trident.

The man—he knew he was male from his scent, regardless of the helm—threw a small disc he'd produced from somewhere, and Fyre increased his speed to evade it as he curved to his right. The object followed and worse, gained on him. In the flashes he had of his foe while he swooped and dodged, he was able to discern the trainer's movements guiding the projectile. He decided that a direct flight at his opponent might be worth a try and folded his wings to dive. After a few seconds, he pulled them out to level into a glide that would drag his claws against the man's face.

He saw the smug smile an instant before his foe produced another of the disks and hurled it. This projectile immediately branched into a lightning net. Fyre had expected one and was ready for it. He belched a wide fog of ice to intercept it and plowed through the frozen strands with barely a deceleration, but his attack missed as his opponent dove and rolled to avoid it.

A sudden pain in his wing heralded the onslaught of flame darts cast by his enemy. He growled at the injury, which immediately started to heal, and swooped in again. If he'd had Cali's strength to draw on, he would have simply collided deliberately with the trainer and clawed him to pieces. But his foe was adept at dealing with Draksa, clearly, and would see that effort coming a mile away.

More objects were airborne now, and the man controlled six of them simultaneously. Fyre flapped to gain height before they could box him in and had to concentrate on avoiding them as they whipped in one after the other. These had spikes rather than nets, and he'd put every dollar Cali had on a bet that they were poisoned. He managed to ice one down and make it fall but was soon on the run, trailing a couple and frantically searching for the others.

Still, he was smarter than most Draksa and almost certainly more so than any this man had faced. He rocketed high and immediately plummeted, twisting and twirling to avoid the objects. His speed left them behind easily, and his spiral made it hard for his opponent to target him with the blasts he fired from his trident.

The impasse ended when the trainer's concentration broke and the discs thudded into the grass around him while he huddled under a shield to protect himself from the impact of an angry Draksa. Fyre blasted the barrier with ice to lock him in and swooped to avoid making impact himself. His moment of satisfaction was broken when the cocoon shattered and icy pellets bounced off his scales. He spun to see another lightning net flying toward him, this one too close to dodge.

Tanyith frowned at his opponent as the woman made a series of gestures like an old-time-movie martial artist. When she finished, she was in a back stance with glimmering shadow blades in each hand that gleamed black and purple. He imagined he could see the malevolence radiating off them. *I hope mine are up to the task.*

He attacked, momentarily amused by the memory of the Malniets telling him that he should allow himself to be vanquished early. *Now it's time to give this one a little of what they got.*

She exploded out of her stance into a leaping kick, and he angled to the side to avoid it. In midair, she pointed both daggers at him and a line of shadow extended from each. He barely interposed his weapons in time, and the shields that sprung from their tips defeated the beams. Focused, he kept the barriers moving with the woman, who sustained the attack until her feet found solid purchase and she threw the blades.

Tanyith flinched and batted them aside but in the interim, she'd summoned another two and closed half the distance between them. *Damn, she's amped up somehow.* He'd tried to learn how to use his magic for speed but had never mastered it enough to sustain it while doing anything else. But what he lacked in finesse, he usually made up for in endurance and sheer bullheadedness. He used a blast of force to launch him up and over the woman, who skidded on the grass as she twisted to face him. In his split-second moment of advantage, he launched a lightning bolt into her stomach, and her armor glowed as it absorbed the magic but apparently, not all the impact. She grunted, nodded at him, and attacked even faster.

His first reaction was to throw a force barrier in her way at ankle height and when she skipped over it, he summoned another at her throat. She crouched to avoid that one too, and he hurled a ball of fire at her head. Unde-terred, she crossed her daggers and shouted, and his attack was sucked into them and vanished in a second. In the next moment, he was on the run again, doing his best to stay out of her range so the unnaturally fast attacks couldn't catch him.

This is not sustainable, he acknowledged as he panted for breath. *I have to try something different.* He slid his hand into the pouch at his waist and grasped the glass orb Invel had given him for a fight long before. The Dark Elf had ensured that he and Cali each had one after the initial battle they'd been intended for, and there hadn't been a reason to use them since. Now, though, it was the only thing he could think of to even the score. *This will totally suck.*

Cali closed her eyes when her light charm triggered and opened them hoping to find her opponent staggering away, blinded. What she discovered instead was that his armor plates were aglow, having absorbed her magic and protected him. The pressure of his sword against her shield had lessened slightly, however, which gave her an opportunity.

Before all her work with Nylotte on controlling electricity and the subsequent experience of merging with the sword, she wouldn't have been able to bifurcate her attention enough to achieve the desired result. She tasked one part of her mind to maintain the shield that protected her from being skewered. With that secured, she used the other to create two bands of force beneath her sufficient to lift her far enough off the ground that she could reach behind her back with the arm nearest him.

Her fingers found the handles of the flat throwing knives and worked them free. Her foe continued to press his sword into her, seemingly focused on overcoming her strength with his. After a moment's pause to stabilize the magic she was already using, she opened a gap in the shield on her left that he hopefully wouldn't be able to see from his angle.

She hurled the knives up at the best angle she could manage and with as much strength as she could generate. The first struck an instant before the second and scraped ineffectively against his chest plate before it fell. The other stabbed into his stomach above his belt and below his armor. The pressure from his sword abated, and she was able to twist and slap the weapon away with hers.

Swiftly, she rolled away and to her feet and raised Defender in a diagonal block. Her opponent yanked the knife free and threw it at her. A subtle shift of her blade deflected the projectile and he grimaced. "Sneaky trick, Matriarch."

"There are more to come," she said and nodded.

"I don't suppose you'll wait for a minute while I take a healing potion."

Cali raised her chin with a smile. "Go ahead. Give it a try and see what happens."

Her opponent chuckled. "Too bad we had to meet this way. I think we would get along."

She shrugged. "You could submit. I'll buy you a drink after—hell, I'll buy you as many as you like."

He shook his head. "I'm afraid I have a job to do." He stalked slowly toward her as he drew a dagger with his offhand and led with the Rivette family sword.

The magic deflector attached to the back of Fyre's compass pendant snapped as the lightning web met its protective aura and shattered both the web and the crystal. He bathed his foe with an ice blast, and his opponent's attempt to evade was only partially successful. The man's left arm and leg were encased and a less restrictive sheen of frost covered the rest of him. He shouted a curse and hurled the trident.

The Draksa couldn't get completely out of the way of the speeding projectile, and its tines scraped along his stomach and sheared through his scales and into his flesh with an effectiveness no other weapon except another of his species' claws had ever done. Clearly, the trainer had excellent resources.

However, he did too. He assumed the man would be able to call the trident back or produce a second weapon, so he avoided the apparent opportunity to counterattack. Instead, he circled toward his adversary's disabled side and forced him to turn to keep him in sight. He continued to circle and waited for a stumble or misstep to give him an opening.

It was a great plan, right up until the moment when the trainer crouched suddenly, shielded himself, and cleared his affected limbs of the ice. Fyre attacked the shield with his breath and claws but was unable to pierce it as the man downed a vial, doubtless a healing potion. As he banked sharply for another run, the man's weapon returned to his hand and he summoned a lightning net, this one dangling from his free palm.

"Enough playing, lizard," he shouted. "It's time for you to learn your place." He swept the trident horizontally before him, and an inescapable torrent of electricity streaked out in a wide cone. Fyre howled as it struck, folded his wings protectively, and plummeted.

Tanyith careened toward the woman, hoping a better option would appear but fairly confident that it wouldn't. His main hand dagger had a double-sized shield on it, and he interposed it in the path of the incoming shadow bolts. His opponent raced forward, equally eager to end things, and he hoped she didn't also have something sneaky planned.

Well, there's nothing to do about it now. He braced himself for the pain to come and squeezed with his left hand, broke the glass, and sliced his palm with the sharp crystals, which were capable of piercing a Draksa's hide. Human skin and flesh offered little resistance.

His adversary tried to dodge at the last moment and cut to his weak side, but he expected it. She stabbed with both daggers and her main hand came up and over to drive the weapon into his back, where it skidded along his shoulder blade before it stopped in the muscle above it. Fortunately, his hand had been in motion before she damaged his arm, and he pressed it and the crystals it contained over her nose and mouth. Her other dagger slid off his shield and dealt a flesh wound to his thigh. The impact of her body against his hurled him away, ripped the dagger out of his shoulder, and hammered his head on the ground.

She landed beside him, and the incomprehension on her face quickly turned to stillness as the crystals she'd inhaled ravaged her insides. With tears of pain seeping from his eyes, he fumbled for his potion and concentrated on staying conscious long enough to take it.

***

When the barrier fell around them, Cali grinned at her opponent and whirled to run toward Fyre's position. *It's time for phase two.*

CHAPTER TWENTY-FIVE

Cali pushed magic into her muscles as she ran to assist Fyre. They had assumed that she would face the strongest of the enemies and their planning had taken that into account. Once the barriers fell, they'd agreed to gather at the centermost position to support each other. She realized that no one was running from Tanyith's position almost at the same moment that she noticed the two bodies on the grass. A brief internal struggle over whether to go to his aid ended when she saw his arm raise while his opponent remained immobile.

She focused on the battle ahead of her. Fyre had landed hard, entangled in a lightning net. His foe now stalked toward him with his trident raised as if he intended to stab it into him. *Not while I'm alive, buddy.* She feared his armor might be the magic-absorbing kind and didn't want to risk finding out. Instead, she snatched and lobbed a grenade and gave it a gentle push with a force burst as it landed. She followed it with the prototype Kayleigh had given her, this one targeted to land near Fyre.

The flashbang exploded almost at the man's feet and the trainer staggered. The disc sucked away the electricity from the net and Fyre surged upright. She was about to follow her sneak attack with a better one when a burst of pain bloomed at the back of her left shoulder and radiated down her arm and into her torso. The shock of it tripped her, and she stumbled and toppled to twist at the last minute and take the impact on her good shoulder rather than her face.

The Draksa snarled and barreled at his foe. The wild swings of his enemy's trident seemed more like reflex or desperation than real violence, and he closed the distance between them quickly. The trainer's armor started to glow and he blasted the man with frost in hopes of stopping whatever he attempted. It took only moments to fully encase him, and Fyre smiled in satisfaction as he admired the ice statue.

Unfortunately, the pleasure was short-lived. The ice melted and the figure stepped forth, steam rising from the still-glowing scales of his armor. *He held that trick back. Clever.* Fyre easily dodged the fire darts the man launched from the tips of his trident and whipped his tail in the fierce attack all Draksa shared. His foe's clumsy attempt to dodge was a testimony to the lingering effects of the grenade, and the swipe cut his legs from underneath him. The trainer landed hard and his head smacked against the grassy earth as his weapon fell from his hand.

He, Cali, and Tanyith had all agreed they'd kill only if

they had to, but he now faced a quandary. The glowing armor seemed to prevent him from icing the man and he didn't have much else to use to restrain him. He looked over to check on Cali's progress because she had zip ties and saw her splayed on the ground with another enemy closing on her position. That made his decision for him.

The Draksa lined up with the man's skull and made a forward flip, landed on his back, and drove his tail down on the figure's helmeted head. The trainer's still form didn't react. It was possible he'd killed him but maybe not. At any rate, he wouldn't be up in time to join the fight. *A claw along the throat would have been a surer route.* He rolled to his feet, his wings unfurled, and took flight toward Cali.

<hr>

Tanyith had downed both the healing potion and an energy potion before he was able to struggle upright. Remembered pain from the wounds lingered, and he shuddered at the reality of what had happened to him. He bent to check on the woman he'd fought, but she was beyond saving. He regretted the necessity but not the choice. *Extreme times call for extreme measures. Besides, she was doing a really good job of killing me.*

He picked his weapons up and slotted them into place before he raced to the other side of the field. Fyre leapt skyward, traveling away from him, and he hoped Cali wasn't in trouble. The thought made him laugh, even at such an inappropriate moment. *When is she not in trouble?*

Cali continued her roll to avoid the man's attempts to stamp on her. Every time her wounded shoulder touched the ground, she gritted her teeth against a scream. *Damn it, I think I'm in trouble.* She scrambled to her feet and managed to bring Defender into play, focused only on blocking while she got her bearings.

She mentally asked the sword if it could heal her, and the matriarch's voice in her head sounded regretful. *That is beyond our ability. We can give you power but you would have to do the healing yourself.* She grimaced as the pain from a deflection rattled through her. *He's even stronger than he was.* To counteract his enhancement, she pushed more magic into her muscles and her shoulder throbbed in agony. Her left hand was virtually useless as that was her damaged arm, but she tried to pull the flap that held her potions open with it anyway.

Fyre saved her. He flashed into sight from above and his claws slashed at her enemy's face. The man dodged with a yell and almost managed to tag the Draksa with his sword as he whipped past. A lightning attack followed quickly, but Fyre was canny enough to already be turning for another pass. She sent a thank you to him, stabbed Defender into the dirt, and swallowed a healing potion and an energy potion in quick succession. After a moment to allow their effects to kick in, she surged into her next assault.

He spun to face her faster than she'd ever seen anyone move. She halted and backpedaled, thrust his sword away with Defender, and summoned her left stick to catch the attacks she wasn't swift enough to intercept with her other hand. With a frown, she reached deeper into the sword, which responded readily to her call. Everything slowed and she was almost able to sneak in an attack now and then. She reached out to Fyre, and the Draksa lent her strength, which allowed her to push her muscles harder. When she managed a riposte, she knew the odds were turning in her favor.

Her relief was short-lived as his speed increased to match hers and grew faster still. *What the hell?* Defender revealed it was privy to her thoughts as the patriarch replied, *He's pulling magic from somewhere.* She cursed inwardly. *So that's what the extra six jerks on their side are for.* Imagining Styrris's smug smirk at the trick infuriated her, but she pushed it down. *Two can play at that game, scumbag.* She extended her magic to find Tanyith and tugged gently at his power, not knowing if it would work or not. A thin trickle came back. It wasn't much but more than she'd had. She sensed Fyre landing somewhere distant from her position to crouch on the ground, and the flow of energy from him increased dramatically.

She countered her foe's attacks but again, couldn't gain an advantage. It was inevitable that he'd win if she didn't do something more. Cali fumbled a block and shouted, "*Scield,*" and the shield charm burned away as it saved her from a fatal blow. She used the protection to launch her attack, and he deflected it with ease. Her thrown stick missed his head, which seemed to jump from one place to another as his speed increased even more.

Backpedaling, she threw her grenades one after the other, trying to get some distance as she pushed all the magic her muscles could hold into them. She let some trickle out from her hand to coil into a lightning whip, and when he emerged from the smoke with singed armor and tears running from his eyes from the gas, she snapped it at his neck. He snarled and arced his sword in a sharp slice to sever the strand of electricity. The feedback surged through her, and she shouted in a mixture of pain and frustration.

Cali registered that voices clamored for her attention, but she'd been too distracted to hear them before. *Let us help you*, the first Leblanc matriarch told her. *Stop resisting.* She frowned as she hadn't tried to resist the sword. *But maybe I do it automatically?* She certainly had a natural aversion to relinquishing control. With a deep breath, she focused inward and let herself submerge into Defender.

Time slowed to a crawl, but she couldn't move to take advantage of it. Numerous voices welcomed her one by one, while an argument took place in the background. She tuned in to the conversation that included three voices, each making the case as to why they were the best answer to her needs. She couldn't tell anything about them from their voices and no visual reference was available. Finally, they came to an agreement, and with a tone of good humor, she heard, *Hold on, Caliste. This will be fun.*

Things snapped into their recent insanely fast tempo but now, her body seemed like it had learned much more about fighting with a sword. She was still in control—or at least it felt that way—but every move she made was a little more precise and thus a little more effective. One part of her brain babbled about possession, remembering Nylotte's warning from what seemed an age before, but the rest of her merely gloried in the thought that she might survive and win freedom for her brother. It hadn't seemed all that likely a few moments before.

She'd taken the offensive and now, her opponent was the one who backpedaled instead of her. His deflections were enough to keep him safe as her sword scraped along the metal plates of his armor but it was apparent that he wouldn't last through a lengthy battle. He seemed to acknowledge that reality after a particular blow almost caught his neck, and he stopped moving and discharged a torrent of lightning from all over his body. The plates acted as conduits or something and the magnitude of the magic was stronger than she'd ever seen. It reached out for her and he pushed in, planning to skewer her while she was distracted by the stunning sneak attack.

The anti-magic deflector crystals exploded on her chest with the intensity of punches but in the face of his rush, she barely noticed them. Unbelievably, he'd left himself open. She crowed within as she whipped Defender at precisely the right angle to shatter his sword, which broke with a strangely beautiful chime. Her momentum allowed her to pivot so his effort to stab her with the broken section that remained attached to the hilt missed, and she drove a force-empowered hook punch into the side of his head. He sagged and fell and didn't rise.

Cali turned to look for other dangers, but only found her teammates, who stood nearby and looked at her like she was an alien. Time resumed its normal pace, and she asked, "What?" Cheers and boos issued from the stands as she walked to her friends.

The man shook his head and turned to Fyre. "She's

some super-swordswoman now. We'll never hear the end of it."

The Draksa nodded. "There's no coming back from this. She'll be so annoying."

She laughed and wrapped them both in a hug. When she broke the embrace and looked toward the royal box, it was empty. With a growl, she ran to the Malniet side of the field, only to discover that what she feared had occurred. The patriarch and his entourage were gone and with them, the prize that had been the whole point of the conflict.

Tanyith put his hand on her shoulder and stepped beside her as Fyre leaned against her legs from the opposite side. "Don't worry. We'll find him or we'll rip his family, his mansion, and anything else he owns apart until we get what you need."

CHAPTER TWENTY-SIX

Ozahl and Danna had viewed the battle from among the crowd but had positioned themselves at the top so they could leap from the structure once the results were known. If Styrris had won, they would have eliminated anyone in the Leblanc mansion and claimed it as their own. But with the patriarch's loss, it was time to finish their attack on the Malniet family.

He had set up a signal for the people they'd hired—a scarlet firework to move against Leblanc and a green one to move against Malniet. Now, he launched the latter into the air, where it reached almost to the top of the dome before it detonated to send streamers of light through the pseudo-night sky. Together, they ran toward their agreed destination and used magic to fuel their endurance so they'd arrive fresh and ready for what lay ahead.

All across the city, mercenaries removed the rest of the Malniet family, those who had been located but they hadn't been able to deal with ahead of time. Their previous efforts had been limited to those on the edges whose absences wouldn't be noticed. But now, the gloves were off and they didn't need to worry about restraining themselves.

They lacked enough hired guns to handle everything, though. And honestly, even if there had been sufficient numbers, Ozahl knew Danna shared his desire to put an end to the Malniet line in person. Not that it was personal, as such. Any house would have done, although this one was probably more deserving than most. Rather, it was a case of wanting to be the author of the final act of the story of their rise to nobility.

They slowed as they neared the mansion. The front gate was open and his people—the mercenaries he trusted most—were in position in front of it. He nodded a greeting. "What's the situation?"

The merc leader, a woman with a notably more muscular build than his own, replied, "The immediate family is inside, along with anyone else who might have been in there when we arrived." The black-uniformed woman and her compatriots would have moved into the area shortly after the Malniet procession left for the arena.

"Excellent." Personally, despite her fitter form, he thought the black uniforms he and Danna wore were more attractive. They had no symbols and no decorations and were merely heavy cloth that blended with the night and belts to hold objects of violence. They even sported the same severe slicked-back hairstyle for the evening. "Did you have to turn anyone away?"

The woman grinned. "A few. They're in your warehouse."

Ozahl nodded. He'd set the mercenaries up to portal any Malniets they found into another warehouse in New

Orleans that he had prepared. People he'd hired there would use sedatives to keep them out of trouble until he was ready to deal with them. He hoped most would select exile. Some, like Styrris, wouldn't have that option because they were too dangerous to control.

"Again, excellent. We'll take care of the folks inside the mansion. Maintain the perimeter. No one comes in, including anyone who says they're our allies unless it's the Champion of New Atlantis." Usha was keeping an eye on House Cormier at the head of a small squad of hirelings in case Brielle's family made the poor decision to rally to the aid of their recently added relatives.

Danna led the way to the front door, which opened at a gesture when she was six feet away. She accelerated and dove into the room, and a series of magical attacks rocketed into the doorway where the attackers had judged she'd be. He ran in after her and hurled force bolts with both hands to catapult two of the four people on the stairs into the walls and down the staircase. Calmly, he conjured a shield to protect himself from the other two's assaults.

His girlfriend had already summoned and thrust her ice spear through one man in a Malniet guard uniform. He recognized belatedly that those he fought also wore the black and silver outfits. She yanked the weapon free, twirled it to intercept a blast of fire from one of the family members, and launched it at the other woman. Her foe looked at the spear in shock before Danna dispelled it and the Malniet fell with a hole through her.

"No fire in my house, you bastards," she shouted and jogged out of the main room.

He banished his shield, blasted the two remaining guards on the stairs, and asked, "This floor first?"

It took them less than fifteen minutes to clear the mansion, but they knew a few people were still missing. Styrris, for one, his bride if she had accompanied him, and the heir, one of the patriarch's children from a previous marriage. Ozahl remembered vaguely that it had originally been a daughter but that something suspicious had happened to her and now, the position was held by a son. If he weren't about to obliterate their house, it was a circumstance he might have cared about. *Worst case, it's one more reason to kill Styrris.*

They'd returned to the entryway, where Danna folded her arms and shook her head with a frown. "We've looked everywhere. We know they didn't portal out because we have people blocking. We know they didn't leave through any of the doors because our mercenaries are watching. Which leaves the important question unanswered—where the actual hell are they hiding?"

The exasperation in her voice was so her that it filled him with affection that escaped in a laugh. "Don't worry, love. We'll find them. No way we've come this far to fail."

"So what do you propose?"

"We're looking for a rat, so we need to think like a rat." He considered where the Malniets might have put a safe room and decided that if he were doing so, he'd probably think of under the house first. Of course, he'd continue to think, but he guessed they would be satisfied with their first inclination. He strode forward down the long hallway and into the big living room, where one of the Malniet cousins was tied to a chair with a gag in his mouth. Two mercenaries stood in separate corners with crossbows aimed at the prisoner. Even if the man had been stupid enough to try some magic to escape, the guards would have shot him.

Ozahl pulled the gag from his mouth. "So, where are the stairs?" The oaf in front of him was not a trained intelligence person capable of keeping secrets. He'd faced several of those and learned how to break them, which made him significantly overprepared for this situation. The look on his subject's face confirmed the existence of the stairs, and the way his eyes flicked left but frantically darted right told him where they were. He patted the man on the cheek. "Good boy. Thanks," he said as he stuffed the gag into the prisoner's mouth again.

He turned to where the captive had first looked. A tall cabinet stood there, filled with expensive-looking sculptures and other art objects. He used telekinesis to tug gently at it, and the large piece of furniture swung out from the wall to reveal a staircase. Danna stepped beside the opening and peered down. "I'll wager you any amount you like that it's trapped."

The mage shrugged. "No bet." He raised a hand and gestured, and the captive Malniet and the chair he was bound to slid across the floor. Their captive screamed into the gag as he tumbled down the stairs and the seat broke under him. Halfway down, lightning sizzled from both walls and intersected at his body. When he reached the bottom, spikes erupted from both sides to turn him into a pincushion. "Not bad, honestly. The physical trap was a nice touch."

His full-body shield positioned an inch away from his skin all around, he led the way down the stairs. Danna followed and employed the same precautions. Their path was blocked by a heavy-looking wooden door, and he decided he'd had enough of subtlety. He attacked it with the biggest burst of force he could muster and it flew inward, plowed into a wall a couple of feet away, and fell forward. He strode onto the door and into the hallway and turned to where Styrris and Brielle sat in comfortable chairs, seemingly unmoved by his entrance.

You people must think I'm an idiot. He stepped forward and shot lightning to his left and right to catch both of the individuals who stood ready to ambush him. His expression glacial, he maintained the attack until they fell and continued it until they lay motionless.

Styrris flinched and from behind him, Danna said, "Oh no. Do nothing or you and your lovely wife are dead, right here, right now."

The Malniet patriarch smiled. "I invoke my right as a noble to be judged by the Empress."

Ozahl sighed. *Of course, he knows all the old rules.* "That doesn't protect your wife," he observed in a conversational tone. "And it's not technically appropriate as you're not being charged with anything in particular."

The older man inclined his head. "Letter of the law, certainly. But the spirit of the law allows it. And, like you've said, unless you also kill my wife, there will be a record of the claim. Do you want to bring the palace down on you? Does Leblanc?"

He laughed and Danna joined him. Styrris looked confused while they indulged in their amusement. When he could finally speak steadily, he replied, "Oh, Caliste didn't send us. We're here of our own accord. Now, shut up for a minute or I'll be forced to render you unconscious."

Ozahl stepped back to Danna and covered his mouth with his hand so the captives couldn't see what he was saying. "Okay, he's not wrong. And he has a fairly good point about the whole Empress judging principle. We probably don't want to start our life as nobles by flaunting that particular law, however stupid it might be."

She mimicked his posture. "And if Shenni says he can go free?"

He shrugged. "Then we kill him later. And while we're at the palace, Usha and our mercenaries will ensure no Malniets remain to support him. We will have defeated them and she won't be able to refuse our petition to replace them."

His partner shook her head. "And why is that better than simply killing them both and waiting it out?"

"It allows us to meet the Empress from a position of strength and proves to her that we've taken over Malniet."

After a moment, she nodded. "Okay, when you put it that way, I'm in."

He lowered his hand and grinned. "Very well. Let's all go see Shenni."

CHAPTER TWENTY-SEVEN

As she strode forward in the center of four guards with Gwyn leading the way, Shenni's mind bounced constantly between several thoughts. It seemed to stick with one until it either ran its course or reached an impasse, only to return to it when the cycle was complete.

The first was her enduring frustration at the success of House Leblanc. The girl's parents had been irritating enough that she'd backed the play that drove them from the city. When they'd appeared in New Orleans and began to cause trouble again, she'd been the one to demand their deaths and even loaned her family sword to ensure the success of the endeavor. In retrospect, delivering the pieces of the Leblanc weapon to curry favor with the houses hadn't been a smart decision.

Acknowledging a mistake cut that thread off very rapidly. Shenni wasn't in the mood for negative self-reflection. *No, I'm in the mood to take someone's head off their shoulders.* The next thought was that she'd rarely been in this part of the palace, if ever. Her appointment needed complete security, which meant a secret entrance into the building and a chamber in a mostly unused wing. The halls and rooms through which they moved were well-kept but not at the level of the spaces she usually enjoyed. She'd bowed to the moment by throwing on one of her least favorite Empress costumes, a martial styled tunic that reached from her throat to her calves with golden buttons from top to bottom.

Senseless irritation over that pushed her to the third thought, which was to wonder why she'd ever courted House Malniet in the first place. Gwyn had warned her—gently, of course—and the other woman's concern that the patriarch was both untrustworthy and too often led by emotion instead of reason had proven valid. "He tries to look big," her seneschal had observed, "because he feels small," and those words had proved prophetic.

Which derailed her onto her fourth thought. *What the hell can I do now?* Lacking an answer to that put her back into the cycle repeatedly, and she'd grown angrier with each turn through the list of failures. When they arrived at their destination—a room she was told was once part of a love nest for a previous monarch—people were already waiting inside.

The entire chamber was ringed by guards who held spears, swords, or crossbows at the ready. Her protectors stayed out of the room to avoid messing up sightlines for the bows. She stopped within a couple of paces of the door, which put her about twelve feet away from the others.

Styrris Malniet, looking as ruffled as she'd ever seen him, sat in one chair. Beside him was his bride, Brielle Cormier, who plainly looked sick. For a moment, Shenni's heart beat in sympathy with the other woman's. Then she recalled that the matriarch hadn't been strong enough to withstand the internal conflict that betrothed her to the Malniet patriarch and the sympathetic moment ended. Their clothes were the same as they'd worn at the arena, which suggested that events had moved fast after that.

Behind them, dressed in black and looking equal parts pleased and annoyed, stood two people. One she recognized from Usha's descriptions and a picture she'd shared—Danna, the Atlantean gang's secondary leader. The other she didn't know. He was tall with brown hair and piercing eyes, and a sense of confidence radiated from him. The woman possessed the same air, Shenni realized, but she expressed it more subtly.

In a rare moment of intelligence failure, Gwyn hadn't been able to discern why these people had requested the immediate audience. The statement that a noble had called for judgment had been enough to set all this in motion without that knowledge, one of the few levers the nobility still possessed to move her to action. It wouldn't do to ignore centuries of precedent. Besides, she was safe. Even if the newcomers suddenly exploded, the invisible shields her best guards maintained around them would keep everyone but the attackers from injury.

She nodded at her guests. "Styrris. Brielle. Who are your friends?"

The former started to speak but a light tap on the back of the head from the man she didn't know silenced him. The woman said, "I'm Danna. This is Ozahl."

Shenni stared at her. "It seems you have a story to tell."

The man laughed. "It isn't a complicated one. Simply

put, Malniet is finished. The family line is ended and we have claimed the properties and statuses they once owned since we are the ones who did the ending. You're looking at your newest nobles, Empress."

The revelation was unexpected, although in retrospect, the scene before her should have told her what was coming. *There's so much on my mind, to be fair.* She addressed her seneschal. "Gwyn, is there precedent for this?" Styrris tried to speak and was rewarded with a harder slap, which would probably have been her response to the interruption too.

The older woman nodded. "Yes, Empress. It was more frequent in Old Atlantis but it has happened here as well. If, in fact, they hold the mansion and other family properties and can demonstrate that they do so unchallenged, the holdings would be legally theirs."

Shenni smiled at the recently wedded noble couple. "Styrris, I presume you have something to say about this?"

He cringed a little as he replied, possibly expecting another strike to the back of his head. "Indeed, Empress. You hold the power to reject their ridiculous claim. Kill them now and all will be as it was. Together, we'll finish Leblanc."

Her appearance at the contest had revealed her position regarding that particular house, so she wasn't worried about the spilled secrets. She could always play it off if the two upstarts decided to make an issue of it. "Gwyn?"

The seneschal shrugged. "Also true, Empress. While it's not technically legal, monarchs have unquestionably taken such actions in the past. It carries the advantage of maintaining the current balance among the Nine." Unsaid was their shared opinion that Styrris had looked for a way to tip that to his advantage for some time, which is what led him to the alliance with Cormier in the person of his bride.

Outwardly, she kept her face impassive as she appeared to ponder the situation. Internally, she laughed at the sight of the pompous patriarch brought low by a couple of commoners. Like Usha's, it was a great story. The new arrivals would sow chaos among the nobles for a time, during which she could analyze the changing power structure and find a way to exploit it. The destruction of the Malniet House—one of the longest-tenured and most powerful of the Nine—would result in dramatic repercussions. She couldn't anticipate them all but was confident she could ride the waves as they appeared.

She sent a mental message to Gwyn. *Do you have an opinion on the matter?*

The other woman's reply was tinged with a little worry and considerable satisfaction. *Styrris is a wretched person. He's earned this outcome.*

The Empress agreed completely. *And yet I probably owe him something, after all.* She nodded and focused on the four in front of her. "I won't intervene in this affair. It is a matter for the nobles. If Malniet is in fact dispossessed, the protocol is clear. In nine days, if you still hold their properties, Malniet will be no more and you will replace them. I suggest you prepare for any number of challenges." In truth, no one was likely to stand up on the fallen family's behalf and she didn't think anyone else was ready to make a move. Plus, the situation would allow for another of her plans to reach fruition. "I will award you a half-hour head start, Styrris, in recognition of what has gone before. I urge you to make your way to safety somewhere other than New Atlantis. Also, before you go, you will give Gwyn the information you owe Leblanc."

He sputtered and she raised a hand. "I have spoken and it is so. Gwyn, see him out." The barriers fell and the guards and seneschal took the patriarch in tow and left the chamber.

To the remaining three, she said, "I will entertain Matriarch Cormier for the duration. You two can discuss details with Gwyn when she returns. You may wait in the hall." They nodded and headed to the door, accompanied by yet more guards. Shenni sat beside Brielle. "So, that didn't work out too well for your house, did it?"

The other woman sniffed but remained silent, a pained expression on her face. The Empress patted her hand. "There, there. Everyone makes poor decisions sometimes. But maybe we can make this one turn out for the best."

CHAPTER TWENTY-EIGHT

Styrris Malniet had raged internally at his reversal of fortunes for hours, which was how long it had taken him to make his way in secret to his destination. He'd planned ahead for the day when something went wrong and had prepared a bolt hole to hide in, but that was only a temporary solution. Never in his wildest estimation had he imagined such a disaster as he now faced.

But it's fixable. I have options. The night had been almost endless, but when the sun rose an hour before, he had readied himself to act. Now, he sailed over the boundary fence on a burst of magic like a common criminal, having compromised the wards surrounding the house long before. It was the only place left for him, and while it wasn't his original plan, it would still work out over time. He'd build a newer, stronger base and continue with his plans to replace the other weaker houses. Styrris took a moment to tug his tunic down to straighten it and ran an absent hand through his hair to push it back. He steeled himself and strode around the corner to present himself to the two guards who were on duty at the mansion's main entrance.

The senior of the two—a woman he recognized from previous visits—nodded at his appearance and seemed unsurprised. *It's to be expected that I was expected.* A back portion of his mind snickered at the wordplay and he stifled it quickly. Madness lay in that undisciplined direction and he wouldn't countenance it. "Patriarch."

"I would see the matriarch."

"Of course." She gestured and the other guard knocked on the doors in a complex rhythm. They opened to reveal the majordomo in a uniform of Cormier green with silver trim. The woman nodded and requested, "Please follow me, Patriarch."

He raised his chin to the proper angle for dealing with a servant and strode after her as she walked deeper into the mansion. The House of Cormier's abode was far less opulent than his, fitting his opinion of them as a lesser family. It was one of the things that made his effort to join with them possible. A stronger opponent would have offered far more resistance.

Styrris was escorted into the fanciest of the house's reception rooms, which wasn't saying much. It featured dark wood walls hung with art he found pedestrian, a thick brown carpet on the floor, and several pieces of leather furniture—a couch, a loveseat, and four wingback chairs. Lamps throughout the room cast a soft glow over everything. It was pretty but lacked personality. *Kind of like my wife,* the voice in his head chittered. Again, he pushed it down vigorously.

The woman in question entered from a different door

than he'd used. She was dressed in dark-green, a hunting dress with a wide belt at the waist and pants and boots beneath. They'd shared a hunt on Oriceran once, and she had proved surprisingly capable. She gestured for him to take the loveseat and sat near him on the couch. *Close but not together.* He took that arrangement as a warning to be on his best behavior, as the power balance in their relationship had momentarily swung to her side.

He gave her a smile and said, "Hello, darling."

She nodded. "Styrris. Where have you been?"

"Here and there." He chuckled. "While this is a setback, it is only that."

The matriarch gestured at the servant who had entered the room. "Tea and whiskey—a service, please." The man bustled away and she returned her attention to him. "How is losing your house simply a setback?" Brielle's tone was neutral but the question was irritating, regardless.

"That's why we married, dear girl, so we can support one another in times of trouble and rise together. The challenge has come sooner than expected and from an unanticipated direction, but we will prevail."

"It sounds logical. However, don't you feel as if your recent decisions have made the situation more difficult, rather than less? For instance, the last leverage you had against Leblanc was the secret you held, and you've given that up to the palace. That kind of poor decision making is unlike you."

The doubt in her tone left him unsettled—as if important things were slipping away. He nodded. "Had I surrendered that, you would be correct. However, since Shenni reneged on her end of our deal, I didn't feel the need to obey. We still hold an advantage over that damn girl and her friends. One that will give us her house if she wishes to save her pathetic brother."

The servant who returned with the tea was a different one, and he was careful to not meet the man's eye. He'd planned to move on Cormier for years and had inserted one of his most skilled and least recognizable relatives onto her staff. His agent had standing orders to find a way to be close whenever he was present and received a steady flow of income as a reward for his actions and the information he shared. Because of him, the patriarch had known for months before it happened that an offer to wed the matriarch was in the works. The man set the service between them, poured the bitter brew and the warming liquor into cups, and withdrew to stand at the back wall.

Brielle lifted the cup to her lips, sipped, and returned it to the tray with a sigh. "I'm sorry to hear you say that, Styrris. I guess I'd hoped that in the end, some honor remained in you. But apparently not."

He scowled at her impertinence. "Be that as it may, you will do your duty per our arrangement. The first step is to name me patriarch of House Cormier and step back to allow me to do what has to be done."

She shook her head. "No, I'm afraid not. You see, the one who made that deal with you has selected exile—as have many members of your family—in order to save their lives. Now, I make the decisions for Cormier, regardless of any arrangement you may have thought you had. And before you try to object, the Empress supports my position."

Styrris's hands clenched involuntarily as he imagined

throttling the woman. He kept his gaze locked on hers because if he looked at his man in the room, he might not be able to resist giving the eye blink pattern that would communicate a request for her quick demise. That moment wasn't yet at hand. He crossed his legs, stretched his left arm along the back of the loveseat, and rested his right on the armrest. "So what is your desire then, Matriarch?"

"Actually, there's someone who wants to talk to you." She turned to look at the door and he followed her gaze as Caliste Leblanc walked through it.

Cali had listened from the hallway for only a minute, not wanting to be seen by the servants who had attended the couple. She hadn't had the highest of hopes when she'd confronted the matriarch at the crack of dawn, but it had been an option she couldn't leave untried. Her shock at finding Brielle receptive to her entreaties had been complete.

But it wasn't nearly as intense as the shock that over-took Styrris's face at her entrance. The servant against the wall flinched but she didn't react. At Brielle's request, she had left her weapons in an outer room, having first sent Fyre to retrieve Invel to watch over them. The Draksa hadn't been permitted entry but circled over the estate hidden by a veil. She'd known Styrris was close before the guards had.

She grinned. "Hey, Styrris. I couldn't help but overhear the part where you lied to the Empress. But you lost, despite your constant efforts to cheat. This is where you make good on your commitment and tell me what I need to know."

He looked from her to his wife and back to her without speaking. His eyes narrowed. "You planned this?"

Cali shook her head. "I stupidly thought you'd honor your word. We're merely in improvisation mode, now. But it looks like me and mine are better at it than you and yours." She ran a hand down the front of her dress to remove a piece of lint she'd noticed. The outfit from her mother's wardrobe displayed subtle black patterns on a black base with turquoise spots and slashes here and there. Her belt with the compass buckle finished the look nicely. She regretted not having taken Kayleigh up on the hidden knife for her boots.

The man nodded. "And then you'll go?"

"And then I'll go and leave you two to…well, whatever it is you'll do." She didn't think it would work out as he planned but there was no reason to mention that.

The patriarch stiffened as if he'd made an important decision. "It's hidden in my house—in a safe in the basement room. I can tell you how to get there."

She nodded in false concentration. "The staircase with the traps to the false safe, which is also trapped. Right. See, the problem is that I know you're lying. It turns out that when you spend your evenings alone in the den before the fire, you talk to yourself. Your secrets—like this fake answer—aren't so secret." Her face hardened. "I don't want to have to do this the ugly way, Styrris. But I'll do whatever I need to do to get that information. Up to and including having a friend of a friend cut you to ribbons until you give it up."

The man turned to stare at the servant and the man blurred into action. She knew from the listening device that someone loyal to him was present in the house and had assumed it was the attendant when she'd noticed him. Even if he wasn't, preparing as if he was had no downside. He yanked a pair of long slender needles from his sleeves as she turned toward him. Styrris's agent moved faster than he should have, doubtless due to magic, and she couldn't risk a magical counter in case he was immune to it as so many of her recent enemies seemed to be.

Her attacker took a direct path to her, which kept him out of range of the matriarch and Styrris. By the time he reached her, the bracelet on her left arm had transformed into her fighting stick and she whipped it at his leading hand and the needle he extended toward her face. His bones shattered and the metal object spun away. She assumed it was poisoned because otherwise, it was a highly ineffective choice of weapon.

Before he could recover, she dropped the stick, used her left hand to push him onward, and grasped his broken hand with her right. She yanked him forward and redirected his momentum to rotate him into the wall closest to her. He fell with a groan, and she stamped her boot on his other hand to be sure he couldn't retrieve either of his fallen weapons.

Cali turned to check on Brielle and saw the Malniet patriarch—*former Malniet patriarch since that house doesn't exist anymore*—close his fingers over one of the dropped needles. His wife recoiled with a shout of alarm, and the girl saw in an instant what was about to happen. Either he'd murder the woman, become the de facto head of Cormier, and probably blame it on her, or he'd kill himself out of spite to deny her the knowledge she needed if he felt he'd lost. It was guaranteed that he would be wearing something to protect him from magic because people like him always ensured their safety above all else.

Reflex took over and she summoned a wall of force with her left hand to block him from Brielle. She yanked the buckle off her belt and popped the blade out with her right, a move she'd practiced a hundred times since she'd received it to the annoyance of those around her during meals and conversations. To give it a spin, she hurled it sidearm and aimed at the patriarch's hand, which was already easing the needle toward his body. She managed a nudge of force to adjust its trajectory and wished for what had to have been the millionth time that she had any aptitude at all for telekinesis.

It sliced along his arm and he cried out and dropped the needle. She launched forward and punched him in the solar plexus, retrieved the zip-ties she'd slipped into her boots, and secured him. As she drew a relieved breath, her legs turned wobbly and she sat heavily on the table and barely avoided the tea service. Brielle cleared her throat and said, "Thank you, Matriarch Leblanc."

"No problem. But I hope your taste in men improves. I guess I'll have to make good on that threat. I'll never understand why people have to suck so much." She shook her head. "All this for power and glory? Some of you nobles need a hobby."

The other woman laughed. "Some of we nobles, you

mean." A smile spread across her face. "To your points, first, my taste in men has already improved." She gestured at one of the guards who had burst into the chamber at her cry of fear and said, "Admit him." A moment later, a tall man in an expensive business suit entered the room. "Matriarch Leblanc, meet Vinton Rivette, my fiancé."

"What is this nonsense?" Styrris sputtered.

She turned to him and her smile widened. "Hush, Styrris. The Empress has chosen not to recognize our marriage. It's as if it never was. Vinton is an old friend and a much-improved choice for a husband."

Cali could have cheered at the sick look that spread across the defeated patriarch's face. *It serves you right, you bastard.*

The newly confident Brielle's next words were even better. "And you don't need to cut him up. I know where the real safe is and the combination to it so you won't have to worry about any traps. You see, he talks in his sleep too. Many old men do, I'm told." She raised an eyebrow at Styrris. "Vinton doesn't, though."

They had to stuff a handkerchief in the man's mouth so his raging wouldn't interfere with their laughter, which was loud and long.

CHAPTER TWENTY-NINE

Cali made her way to the bedroom that held the hidden passage at the head of a procession. Fyre paced at her side and Emalia walked behind her, followed by Invel, Zeb, and Scoppic. Tanyith brought up the rear, talking softly with Jenkins. A thread of magic released the concealed door and she stepped into her brother's chamber with Defender in its scabbard and grasped in her left hand and the spell to counteract the magical poison on a sheet of fragile parchment in her right.

Because of course, the idiot Malniets would use the oldest, most traditional route they could find.

Getting it hadn't been difficult once Brielle had revealed her secrets. She had asked what the Cormier matriarch wanted in exchange but apparently, leaving Styrris in her possession was enough for her. *Justice, I suppose.* She tried not to think about what form that justice might take.

Ozahl, Usha, and Danna had been more than willing to

let her take what she needed. Cali sensed a little tension among them but it didn't particularly concern her. The Leblanc mansion was secure and Zeb and Invel were making plans to add even more magical defenses to those already present. She and her brother would be well-protected before anyone returned to New Orleans.

An orb floating in an upper corner provided the only illumination for the bare stone room. The heavy sarcophagus dominated the small chamber, and she moved to the far end of it. The unadorned white object was shaped like the figure trapped beneath it but lacked any detail beyond the general form. It seemed cold and impersonal.

She remembered having to push the lid off on her previous visits but today, she had help. "Emalia, could you move the lid?"

Her great-aunt didn't reply, only gestured. The top of the sarcophagus floated aside to reveal her sibling within. Atreo was sealed beneath a force shield that shifted and pulsed in changing colorscapes. Again, she found it shocking how similar his features were to her own. She took a deep breath and spoke barely above a whisper.

"My brother was locked in here to preserve his life from a poison that would have shredded his mind. His body has continued to grow while the field halted the progression of the poison. He was frozen as a child." That wasn't the right word, but it was all she had. "There's no telling how he will emerge from this but it has to be better than being trapped here."

Cali sniffed against the tears that welled in her eyes. It had been a long road to this moment and the precipice of fulfilling her parents' plan to save their other child. Fyre, who had leaned against her since the moment they'd stopped walking, sent her emotional reassurance and magical strength. What would come next was impossible to predict, and everyone present stood ready and willing to assist. She couldn't have asked for a more perfect scenario to awaken her brother, except to have Elisinia and Thomas Leblanc beside her.

With a deep breath, she steadied herself. She handed the parchment to Emalia and drew Defender from its scabbard. Her connection to the sword activated quickly, and the memory of how to undo the stasis spell came to her in an instant. *Can it really be that simple? Simply reach out and touch it?*

Fyre spoke into her mind, a testimony to her thinking loudly once again. *Sure. Simple. You only need the right blood, the right sword reconstructed from shards spread all over the place and guarded by everything up to and including zombies—and, oh yeah, to get said sword to accept you without possessing you and eating your brain. Which kind of makes it a zombie too if you think about it."*

Her mouth quirked into a smile and the moment turned from fear to hope. She nodded her thanks and extended her hand. When it met the field, a ripple of turquoise spilled from her fingers, spread, and bounced off surfaces as it increasingly replaced the other colors. When they were gone, it transformed into a shower of sparkles that flowed toward the ceiling and vanished. Her brother took a halting breath but didn't open his eyes.

She held the parchment out with her right hand and

spoke the words on it as she sent her magic into the sarcophagus until she imagined it spilling over the brim. Her voice gained strength as she repeated them over and over, trying to cover him and suffuse him with the power. Suddenly, she fell inward as she had with Defender when she'd first met those inside.

Instead of a barren landscape, though, she found herself in her favorite of the house's many dens. Two wingback chairs stood opposite one another on either side of a gaming table that held a chessboard. A game was in progress, based on the position of the pieces, but she had no idea who was winning or losing. She glanced up and couldn't take her eyes off the person across from her.

The image of Atreo leaning back in the seat bore a smile that she recognized from her mirror. His hair was less red than hers—more copper-colored—and lacked the curl. The clothes he wore looked like what she'd seen in her father's wardrobe in the mansion. He nodded, and his voice sounded exactly as warm and resonant as she'd expected it would be. "You got your curls from Mom. I got this from Dad." He waved at his head.

"You can hear my thoughts?"

He shrugged. "Thoughts and speech are essentially the same in here."

Cali looked around and noticed that the edges of the room wavered slightly, proof of their unreality. Fyre was present too, she discovered, curled on a couch a few feet away and to the side. "Where are we? Your mind, I guess?"

He nodded. "Part of the magic my parents—our parents —left was this place. They did it so I could read and learn while my body grew. I don't know how they did it." He laughed with no trace of concern in the sound. "I don't know how they did any of it, honestly. I'm merely glad they did."

While he talked, Cali had a creepy sensation of familiarity that she didn't understand. He laughed at her again. "I know, right? It's like we've been together for some time, even though I've been essentially a mummy. But fortunately, not a zombie." He paused, raised an eyebrow, and grinned widely. "Have you worked it out yet?"

Her mouth dropped open and she stared at Fyre. He opened an eye, snorted, and rolled onto his back with his paws in the air. She remembered Nylotte's words about the Draksa from long, long before. "There's something off about this one."

She shook her head. "Are you telling me that you and Fyre are the same person? Er…being?"

He laughed again. "No, nothing of the sort. But I have been…uh…" He paused and shrugged. "Riding along might be the best word. For a time after I was stilled, our parents communicated with me a little. Emotions, that kind of thing. One day it stopped, and I went looking for them. I found him instead and he accepted me. I'm not sure he ever consciously knew I was there but I was able to watch things when he was awake."

Mirth flowed through her from the Draksa, but it was at the new revelation, not a signal that he'd known. That would have felt different. "Good. It'll make getting to know each other for real all the easier. So what do we do now?"

The figure across from her shrugged. "I have to imagine

it will take my body some time to return to consciousness. Until then, we can visit like this. And, if he'll let me, I'll keep hanging out with Fyre. We won't be able to talk or anything, but at least I'll know if you're well."

Cali grinned. "I can't wait. Whatever is ahead, I'm glad we'll be together for it."

CHAPTER THIRTY

In the former Malniet mansion, Danna sat with Ozahl and Usha in the den, which had been cleansed of the Leblanc listening device and was now fully secure. Mercenaries patrolled the grounds, and Ozahl had spent hours ensuring that the wards protecting the premises were as powerful as they could be. It was necessary given the possibility that someone would try to take from them what they'd taken from Styrris and his family.

"So, with this done," she said, "we have a question that remains."

Usha nodded. "Leblanc."

"They seem to be in a favorable position at the moment," Ozahl replied. "Public defeat of their enemies, all their allies present in the city, and a whole host of guards patrolling."

She shrugged. "None of which would stop us if we wanted to do it. Which leads our conversation once again to the beginning. Should we?"

Her boyfriend gestured for Usha to speak. The Champion of New Atlantis reclined in her large wingback chair and swirled the crystal tumbler of whiskey in her hand. The clinking of the ice cubes was barely audible over the crackling flames from the fireplace. Finally, she laughed darkly. "Why do I think that despite appearances to the contrary, that house is probably more dangerous than any of the other seven we might choose?"

Her companions joined her laughter. He said, "She has proven to have more lives than a whole clowder of cats, that one."

Danna took a sip of her bourbon and shook her head. "You'd almost think she was born under a lucky star or something. Things seem to go her way more often than not." She stretched her neck and sighed. "Look at everything we threw at her. Not to mention what the Malniets did."

Ozahl nodded. "I tried several ways to try to take her off the field. They all failed."

Usha shrugged. "So, with all of that stacked against us, it seems like it would be the height of stupidity to target her again, don't you think?"

"I agree," she replied, followed a moment later by Ozahl. She continued, "Now what? Simply relax here and enjoy the plunder of the Malniets while we decide what we want to do next?"

Her former boss shook her head slowly. "I think I'll use my Champion's house for something different since I have a place on the grounds to live." She'd accepted their offer of one of the outbuildings on the property. When the time came that their claim was formally recognized, Usha would be named their heir, pending children, of course.

"What's that?"

The other woman grinned. "It seems to me that our dear Empress Shenni has become entirely too comfortable within the thick walls of her palace. She's forgotten what it means to be the caretaker of the people. I aim to remind her."

Ozahl chuckled. "And how will you accomplish that?"

"A little extortion here, a few threats there. New Atlantis has never really had a criminal underworld and it seems like it's past time for one. I'll be kind of an undersea Robin Hood—take from the rich, share with the poor, and give the local rulers as many ulcers as possible."

Danna laughed. "She'll know it's you."

He shook his head. "Knowing and being able to prove it are different things. Especially when you have friends with certain skill sets." He gestured at his body and his features morphed into a copy of Usha's. "This outlaw can literally be in two places at the same moment." He waved again and turned into himself.

"So, are you saying you'd support that effort?" Usha asked.

He nodded and his partner gave the other woman a smile. "Being a full time noble has to be boring. A little side action would be perfect to keep us sharp." She paused, then said, "So we're agreed. Leblanc continues without our interference. Maybe one day, we can count them among our allies. And we work on making Shenni's life as difficult as possible."

Ozahl raised an eyebrow. "Who knows? Someday, instead of being the patriarch of House Cudon, I'll ascend to the throne. Emperor has a nice ring to it."

Danna sighed and shook her head. "No monarchy for you. You may be my consort, both when I'm matriarch and when I'm Empress."

Usha laughed and tossed her drink back. "Now that's a plan I can get behind." She refilled her glass and lifted it in a toast. "To House Cudon."

They clinked glasses and settled in for the first of many nights of comfortable conversation about suborning the rule of the current Empress.

Cali and Shenni met in the Empress's private office. The seneschal offered her a drink but she declined, preferring to get the necessary discussion over with, and the older woman faded into the background. The monarch sat behind her desk and leaned back, looking smug in her fancy royal gown.

She had worn the uniform she'd fought in, minus the weapons. They'd been smart enough to take her belt, as well, but she would have surrendered it voluntarily. Her safety was assured at the moment by virtue of her fame. There would be an outcry if the one who'd destroyed House Malniet suddenly disappeared while meeting with the Empress, especially given the signaling of her favor toward them at the arena. Besides, her allies were ready to make the trouble happen if it didn't occur of its own accord.

She didn't need to mention any of that to the woman across the desk. Empress Shenni was a political animal and had doubtless calculated all the angles before she allowed her to walk in the door. She smiled and nodded. "Congratulations, Matriarch Leblanc, on your victory."

"Why thank you, Empress. It's too bad you were gone at the end. I would have enjoyed receiving your accolades then."

The woman waved a hand to dismiss the concern. "I have many demands on my time, you know. I would say the outcome would be enough to keep any of the rest of the Nine from challenging your house anytime soon."

"One can hope. I feel confident that House Cudon will be a strong ally going forward. I also hear that House Cormier has formed a new alliance."

Shenni nodded. "Yes, a man in the main line of my former house will join them. It should be a good pairing." Her tone revealed that she'd been behind the move and was happy with its success.

"May I ask you a question?"

The Empress laughed. "Only one? Of course."

"Why did you have my parents killed?" She was proud of herself for asking it without screaming.

Her hostess shrugged. "They were a nuisance. If they had stopped causing trouble when they left the city, they would have had no more retaliation from me. But they chose to oppose my efforts there as well so they earned my wrath."

Cali kept calm only by virtue of her connection to Fyre. The Draksa was perched on top of the palace and sent her calming waves, reminding her that she needed to maintain her poise as best she could. "Then why not kill me now and finish the job? Surely if you hated them enough to loan your family's sword to destroy mine, and then hated me enough to do it again in the recent battle, you must want to."

The monarch laughed dismissively. "Let me speak frankly for a minute. I didn't hate your parents. They were a problem and I solved it. I don't hate you but you are also a problem. If it wouldn't create a firestorm of unrest to kill you out of hand, be assured that I would. But, since that is the almost certain outcome, you get to live. For now."

"So that's it? They were a problem so they died?"

Shenni nodded, and Cali shook her head and stood slowly, wary of whatever defenders the other woman might have watching. "Well, then, I guess I can promise that I'll be a problem for you too. But killing me will be harder since I have allies they didn't."

Her adversary raised her glass in a mock toast. "To the game ahead, then."

Cali strode from the room, the seneschal on her heels. When she reached the entrance, she turned to the other woman. "Oh, I forgot to mention one last thing. Maybe you could let her know for me."

Gwyn nodded. "Of course."

"I collected the shards of her house sword and gave them away to folks who don't have particularly good feelings toward her. Tell her I hope she has fun trying to find them."

She turned and headed home with a smile on her face. *A game is it, you wench? Okay, Shenni. Let's play.*

CHAPTER THIRTY-ONE

Cali snarled in frustration. "Get the hell down from there before you break your head, idiot." The atmosphere in the Drunken Dragons Tavern was particularly raucous for a Monday night. After the events in New Atlantis, she had felt the need to get away and be somewhere familiar. *And, I have to admit, a drunken wizard standing on the table delivering lines from Hamlet is, unfortunately, familiar.*

Accompanied by a round of cheers for him and heckles for her, the white-bearded magical took her hand and climbed onto the floor. He patted her on the shoulder, sat, and began to talk to his friends as if nothing unusual had happened. Which, of course, was par for the course in Zeb's establishment, where the strange was routine.

She collected a tray full of empty glasses and headed to the front for refills. Tanyith and Kendra sat in their usual seats at the edge of the bar, and the detective kept the one next to her clear so that when Cali made it back there, she had somewhere to sit. She slid the tray to Zeb with a smile.

"Get to work, old man. We have thirsty customers out there."

He shook his head and took the tray, grumbling something that was doubtless uncomplimentary under his breath. She turned to Kendra and grinned. "I don't think I've thanked you yet for letting me borrow your boyfriend. He was very useful." She wiggled her eyebrows theatrically so they wouldn't miss the entendre.

The detective rolled her eyes. "If I was still worried you might have designs on him, that right there killed it. No one I've ever met would have the patience to put up with you."

Cali stuck her tongue out at the other woman. Fyre's laughter sounded in her head and she sent, *You can shut up, lazybones,* to him. A snort emerged from behind the bar but he didn't otherwise react. She wondered if Atreo was with him at that moment and was entertained by their antics. It was a good thought and she hoped so.

The tray returned fully loaded, and she headed into the crowd again. The rest of the night passed in a happy blur of work. Zeb stayed open a little late because his patrons seemed like they wanted to linger. "It's a good sign," he'd observed. "Things are getting back to normal around here."

"There's nothing normal about you, buddy," she'd quipped, which made everyone in earshot laugh.

Now, with the customers shooed out the door and the locks thrown, Cali was able to fully relax for the first time in what seemed like months. Zeb pulled glasses of his special brew—a hard cider with hints of blackberry—put them in front of each of them, and took one for himself.

"So, will you be up here doing your job a little more often from here on out?" he asked.

She nodded. "I hope to. I'll have responsibilities down there, of course, and once Atreo is up and moving there will be more, but I don't want to leave this behind. I feel like myself here."

Tanyith grinned. "From waitress and student to noble matriarch. That's quite a change. It would take some getting used to."

"Definitely. So what will you do? Go back to Trevilsom and serve out the rest of your sentence?"

He snorted and coughed on his drink. "Uh, no, I'm good, thanks. I guess I'll help Zeb out when you're not around. And maybe have a conversation with the new leaders of House Cudon about their plans for the Malniets in exile. Someone has to keep an eye on those bastards."

She laughed at the image that jumped into her head of him on a horse with a big hat. "Sheriff Tanyith, huh? Keeping the citizens of New Orleans and New Atlantis safe from the outlaws." When the others had finished laughing, she said, "Seriously, though, it's a great idea. And you're the right one to do it."

The conversation turned to other matters and eventually, Kendra and Tanyith took their leave. She swiveled to face Zeb. "Finally. Lovebirds. Ugh." She made a gagging sound and the dwarf laughed. "So, is everything the same for you, boss? Are you gonna stay here, dish out stew and drinks, and be the voice of reason between the humans and the magicals?"

He shrugged. "Probably." She stared at him in silence until he sighed. "What?"

"It seemed that joining us for those battles suited you."

The dwarf looked thoughtful and replied, "Yeah, you're right. I did enjoy being out there fighting again. It's a little more adrenaline-producing than tending bar."

Cali nodded. "You have good skills in that area. With practice, you could be at least above average. Are you thinking about hitting the road? I couldn't help but notice that you're more or less grooming Tanyith to fill in."

Zeb chuckled and pulled his pipe out, then took several minutes to complete his ritual of filling it and lighting it. After a few puffs, he admitted, "Maybe I am. It's never bad to keep your options open. Speaking of which, will you really settle down in New Atlantis?"

She grinned. "Well, I have to return Ikehara's lucky charm to him in the morning, so I guess I'll work here tomorrow night. After that, there are things to get organized for House Leblanc down there. But once that's all done, who knows? Maybe I'll run for Empress."

He laughed. "I don't think you 'run' for Empress."

"Which makes sense. No one would vote for Shenni. Whatever. The point is, New Atlantis needs a troublemaker and I'm the perfect person to fill that role. Along with Fyre, of course."

"Yeah, I can see that he's the brains of the operation."

"Shut it." She grinned at the dwarf, her heart filled with affection. "On second thought, the Dragons could use troublemaking too. So, when you're here, you can plan on Fyre and I helping out more often than not." She put her hands on the bar and vaulted over to wrap him in a hug. "Whatever I do from here on out, the most important thing to me is being with my friends and family, so count on getting tired of us hanging around."

He patted her back and squeezed her tightly. "That's the best news I've heard in ages."

THE END

If you enjoyed this book, you may also enjoy the first series from T.R. Cameron, also set in the Oriceran Universe. The Federal Agents of Magic series begins with Magic Ops and it's available now at Amazon and through Kindle Unlimited.

FBI Agent Diana Sheen is an agent with a secret...

...She carries a badge and a troll, along with a little magic.

But her Most Wanted List is going to take a little extra effort.

She'll have to embrace her powers and up her game to take down new threats,

Not to mention deal with the troll that's adopted her.

All signs point to a serious threat lurking just beyond sight, pulling the strings to put the forces of good in harm's way.

Magic or mundane, you break the law, and Diana's gonna find you, tag you and bring you in. Watch out magical baddies, this agent can level the playing field.

It's all in a day's work for the newest Federal Agent of Magic.

Available now at Amazon and through Kindle Unlimited

Thank you for reading the final book in the *Scions of Magic* series! I truly hope you enjoyed the ride as much as I did. The love among Cali and her friends was unexpectedly intense at the end. I didn't see it building, and then, as I was writing, there it was. It's always amazing to me how stories take on a life of their own during the writing process.

Reading is a solace for me in difficult times. I've been cranking through rereads of a bunch of old favorites and trying out some new ones over the last couple of months, in between trying to keep my kid occupied and my partner steady. Fortunately, they return those favors in kind. If we have to be socially distant, at least we all (seem to) like who we're stuck with. I hope you're finding your own happy place, wherever it might be.

We're putting a temporary pin in the Federal Agents of Magic / Scions of Magic corner of the Oriceran Universe. There's a lot of awesome Urban Fantasy coming from Martha and Michael, so I'm taking a detour into science fiction for a while. I invite you to come along: all the stuff you love from my books will be in those ones too. Lots of action, lots of snark, lots of humor. Plus spaceships! We're currently in the planning stages, but I'm hopeful the first one will be out by July 2020.

I tried playing Jedi: Fallen Order, and was once again reminded that I am terrible at dark-souls-style games. Just really truly awful. I'll probably go back to it for the story after a while, but have jumped back into a replay of the Witcher 3, which I'm much better at. And the kid and I just restarted The Lego Movie videogame for the third time, I think, which is always a hoot. Looking forward to Birds of Prey (but not willing to pay $20 to rent it).

Devs is turning out to be interesting. A little much in certain ways, but I'm intrigued. *Picard* took a little time to get started, but I've totally got the ST: The Next Generation feels going now. And Patrick Stewart is a treasure, regardless.

I encountered a piece of small and unexpected wisdom yesterday. It was on Twitter, and I can pretty confidently say that rarely does anything that qualifies as "wisdom" happen there, on my timeline at least. But a reminder appeared that we are "Human Beings," not "Human Doings." Some days, the best we can achieve is to be, rather than do. And not only is that okay, it's *desirable*. If you're kind of type-A, like me, you're probably feeling pressured by all the things you're not getting done, with all the time you've suddenly got.

To hell with that nonsense. Exist. Be. Do what you can, and accept that it's enough. Focus on being kind to every-one, and remember that includes *you*, too. Tell that critical voice inside your head that it can just shut the hell up until it has your explicit permission to share again. My kid – nine years old – asked yesterday if we ever heard that voice in our head telling us that we were bad. We explained that it's normal, and that voice lies.

Don't believe the lies. Give yourself a break. Maybe – dare I say – find a good book and lose yourself in it for a while! Take care of those who need you, including your own darn self.

Okay, off my soapbox.

Until next time, Joys upon joys to you and yours – so may it be.

PS: If you'd like to chat with me, here's the place. I check in daily or more: https://www.facebook.com/ AuthorTRCameron. Often I put up interesting and/or silly content there, as well. For more info on my books, and to join my reader's group, please visit www.trcameron.com.

This is week 8 of a different world and it's beginning to feel like we're going to have a varying kind of new normal for the foreseeable future. If you're reading these author notes in the very distant future (or past, which would be way cooler) there was a pandemic and we all retreated to the Victorian era and kept our distance from each other... for the most part.

I've taken up a few hobbies like embroidery that I'm learning from YouTube and sharing with my neighbor over FaceTime (another Martha). I can only do one small piece at a time though or my stitches rapidly go south. I've also taken up cooking – and cooking gadgets are one of my fave things. Air frying is a new passion. But, and I'm not sure how this happened, I recently (accidentally I can assure you despite what the Offspring keeps saying) bought two different large ones. I really don't know what the thinking was behind that other than huge sale, a little bored, they looked really different, and somewhat distracted. I told the Offspring it's for a very big party once we can all gather together again. He said, "Whatever you need to tell yourself, Mom." Apparently, you can even bake in these things. No one tell Anderle. I'll never hear the end of it.

Remember my quest to run a 5k? I was signed up for two different ones in April and May that were both cancelled. Now, the new thing is virtual races. A few friends of mine in Chicago are going to do one with me and then we're going to do brunch over Zoom. Everyone knows that brunch afterward is the best part of running a 5k.

I've also been ordering real books – mostly non-fiction. I have no idea why that's suddenly grabbed my attention, but the latest is The Genius of Birds by Jennifer Ackerman. I love finding out weird stuff about nature like trees actually share nutrients even miles away. Whatever I learn about birds will of course be showing up in a book later.

Tomorrow, my future daughter in law, Jackie Venson will be doing a concert from the garage – she's a great blues guitarist and I hear will be on a magazine cover next month – and some neighbors will come and spread out on the sidewalk to listen.

Besides writing as fast as I can and getting lost in magical worlds – this is life right now. It's actually pretty good and weird and kind of fun in the middle of trying to be careful.

That's the thing about life. I do my best to fit myself to the present circumstances instead of insisting that circumstances fit themselves to me. When I remember to do that, very cool stuff keeps happening. Okay, I'm off to go fry up something really big. More adventures to follow.

JOIN THE ORICERAN UNIVERSE FAN GROUP ON FACEBOOK!

Facebook Here: https://www.
facebook.com/TheKurtherianGambitBooks/

www.ingramcontent.com/pod-product-compliance
Lightning Source LLC
Chambersburg PA
CBHW050240110726

47898CB00007B/2211